The Bearmouth:
A Collection of Hunting Tales

by Brian Rae

ISBN: 978-0-9863297-3-9 (print)
ISBN: 978-0-9863297-4-6 (ebook)

Cover photo: Mark Nichols, Manhattan MT

Book and cover design, prepress specialist:
Kathleen Weisel, Bellingham, WA (weiselcreative.com)

Dedication

T hese stories are dedicated to my loyal friend and hunting partner, who over the years enriched my life with indelible hunts, and to his well-trained horses, who transported us through incredible wilderness and at times unimaginable conditions.

Contents

Bedded Down 1

A Swifter, Kinder Death 11

Importance of Knowing Your Rifle 23

Majestic Buck In Bobcat Pass 35

Scavenger 45

Dinner Date 59

All-Nighter 71

The Bear Den 85

First Bull 93

Too Smart For His Hitches 117

The Old Trapper's Cabin 129

Acknowledgements 155

Bedded Down

B uck Wiley lit a fire in the free-standing wood stove in the ranch
house, then plopped into his old easy chair exhausted from the
day's hunt. It was late afternoon by the time he led his horse Patriot
out of the woods, removed the two meat sacks full of elk meat from
the orange pannier, and fed Patriot some well-deserved grain after
removing her saddle and tack.

Buck was famished but too tired for the moment to get out of his
chair and fix any dinner. He looked up at the seven point elk antlers mounted on the living room wall and let the day's extraordinary
events run through his mind....

Roughly three inches of snow had fallen during the night, but the
stars were now out when Buck shut off the switch to the spot lights
in the tack house, and led Patriot out of the corral. *Perfect conditions*!
He saddled up and headed for the trail leading south from the ranch
toward the high country. *The elk should be down lower this morning, and
it will be easy to cut fresh tracks in this snow....* "I think we'll hunt the
area southeast of Tyler Creek," Buck said aloud to Patriot, riding her up
the cold north-facing gulch. "But we'll stick to the roads this morning
because of the snow." The slopes of this drainage area were steep, but
several tiers of logging roads had been cut into their flanks, making

for easy travel and good visibility of the relatively open hillsides.

Even though his wife and friends would urge him to not hunt alone, especially on horseback, Buck preferred to hunt by himself. He enjoyed riding alone with his horse, scanning the beautiful terrain for game, especially bull elk. He'd shot many big ones over the years, including the monster seven point, whose massive antlers were now proudly displayed on the living room wall in his ranch house. He loved the mixture of excitement, challenge, and fear of the unknown, but he knew from experience how quickly things can happen when you're riding a horse through rugged wilderness.

After a 30 minute climb, he stopped on a logging road well below the area he usually hunted, to give Patriot a rest. "Good job, girl!" he praised patting her on the neck. "You'll be happy to know that this is as high as we're going to climb this morning." She was panting hard from the steady climb through the snow, expelling plumes of steam into the frigid air. After her breathing slowed, Buck reined her down the road toward the southwest. "You can walk nice and easy now."

Rounding one bend, he could see the red blinking light atop the radio tower across the drainage area on Tyler Point. With the exception of Patriot's muffled steps in the snow and the rhythmic squeak of the saddle, it was silent. There was now enough light to make out details on the slopes below them and above them.

It wasn't until three bends later, that Buck spotted the fresh tracks on the road. As he neared them, he could see that they were elk tracks—big elk tracks heading downslope across the road. *Probably at least a 5 point!* Stimulated and extra alert now, he dismounted and walked over to the edge of the road and noted the direction the tracks were going. "This is too steep for us, Patriot; let's find an easier way to head down that way."

Buck knew from experience that you don't directly follow an elk's tracks or you'll just push the animal farther ahead of you. Rather, you move a ways either to the left or right of the tracks; then head the same direction the elk is traveling, so, feeling safe, it'll bed down.

Walking ahead of Patriot, her lead rope in his right hand, he led her a bit farther down the road until he spotted a safer place to walk downslope. After descending a short distance, he walked to his right just far enough over so he could see the elk's tracks. Buck and Patriot continued downslope keeping some distance from the tracks, but verifying from time to time, the direction the elk was headed. *Perfect! The thermals are coming our way—he won't be able to smell us!*

After walking for about 15 minutes, Buck noticed that the elk tracks slowed and meandered a bit. *He's looking for a place to bed down.* He led Patriot over to a tree and secured her lead rope. He removed his orange hunting vest and placed it over his saddle, so another hunter wouldn't mistake her for an elk. He removed his 30.06 from the scabbard and proceeded very slowly peering downslope for the slightest movement or out-of-place color.

After he'd walked about 100 yards, he saw a slight movement downslope and to his right. He took a few very slow, deliberate steps to his right and squared his shoulders to where he'd seen the movement. There, behind a fallen tree trunk about 60 yards downhill from him, he saw the tops of the bull's antlers move ever so slightly above the log. He knew from experience that bulls typically bed down in front of a downed tree, and face downhill, so they can check out the slope below them, while being well-hidden from above.

Even with a lucky shot through the top edge of the log, Buck knew his first shot would not be fatal. The bull would quickly stand up to flee; so his second shot would have to be true. A miss or a non-lethal shot would allow the large bull to take off running downhill, for God only knows how far. He raised his rifle and aimed at the very top edge of the log in the center of the antlers. He released the safety, took a deep breath and held it...**BOOM!** Buck quickly ejected the spent casing and rammed another shell into the chamber. Just as he'd predicted, the bull quickly stood up facing downhill, turned slightly to its right. Buck placed the crosshairs behind the elk's exposed right shoulder and fired. **BOOM!** He knew it was a lethal shot, as the bull hesitated briefly as if stunned. Buck quickly fired another round at the same spot but the bull disappeared from Buck's view. *Damn! He* *shouldn't go too far.... When he falls, I hope a tree or stump keeps him from rolling to the bottom!* Buck drew an "arrow" in the snow with his right foot and hustled back up the hill to get Patriot.

"We got him, Patriot! Let's hope he didn't go far!" Buck reloaded his rifle just in case the bull was still alive, slid it back into the scabbard, and led Patriot down to the "arrow." Once there, they proceeded to the log where the bull had bedded down. On the other side of the log, Buck could see the packed and partially thawed snow where the bull had lain, as well as the churned-up area where it stood up to escape. Red speckled blood dotted the snow telling Buck that one of his shots had hit a lung. Smelling the elk now, Patriot was a bit reluctant to step over the log. Buck tugged on his lead rope. "Patriot, come!"

The steady bloodtrail was easy to follow in the snow and after about 100 yards, Buck could see where the bull had stumbled, hit the ground, and begun his downward tumble. The snow and brush looked like they'd been leveled by a large boulder. Unfortunately for Buck and Patriot, there was no large tree or stump in its pathway to stop its descent. Buck could see from where he stood that the bull had rolled quite a ways farther downslope into a thick grouping of short, bushy fir trees. Holding onto Patriot's lead rope, he zigzagged across the slope as he descended to maintain footing, yet, despite his careful efforts, still slipped and fell onto the snow a few times. Each time, he got up quickly in case Patriot slipped as well.

The bull's momentum carried it about 15 yards into the brushy firs. Some branches had caught the bull's antlers securing the head. It lay on its left side. Its nose faced upward unnaturally; the tongue hung out the side of its mouth. Just to be safe, Buck touched the muzzle of his rifle to the bull's open eye—nothing.

"We're going to have to pull it out of this stuff a ways to work on it, Patriot," Buck said unbuckling one of the saddlebags. He first removed a hatchet and began severing the branches that secured the antlers. As he did so, the elk's head turned more in line with its body. Replacing the hatchet, Buck removed some rope from the same saddlebag and tied one end around the base of the antlers. Grabbing the loose end, he mounted Patriot and wound the end around the saddle horn. "Okay, girl, let's pull this guy outta here." When the rope tightened, Patriot strained against it. Her right hoof slipped on the snow, but she quickly adjusted and began to move the large bull. "Whoa!" Buck commanded when the bull was out of the thick firs and into a small open area. "Back," he added, to create some slack in the rope. "Good girl!" he praised patting her on the neck. He released the rope from the saddle horn and tossed the end onto the snow.

After dismounting, he taped his hunting tag to the antlers and untied the pannier strapped to the back of the saddle. "Okay, let the fun begin," he said securing Patriot's lead rope to a tree several feet from the elk.

Buck had field dressed and skinned many elk and deer on his own, but with today's cold, snowy conditions, he wished he had a hunting partner to secure the elk's legs while he worked to remove the gut ball. Today, he'd have to use some baling twine to stabilize the legs while he did the field dressing. Using a "trucker's hitch" knot that he'd learned from his dad when he was a boy, he tied one hind leg to a nearby low-growing fir; the other hind leg to a rock protruding out of the snow.

Straddling the bull, Buck "unzipped" the bull with his sharp hunting knife; then, using his bone saw, cut through the breastplate up to the neck. Bent over the bull, he began the messy process of releasing the innards from the carcass. Several times, Buck had to stand up straight and lean backwards to stretch out the tense muscles in his back. It didn't take long, however for his hands, warmed by the elk's organs, to turn cold when exposed to the frigid air. Resuming the messy job brought warm relief.

About 25 minutes later, Buck rolled the gut ball to the side of the bull. He released the knots securing the twine so Patriot could pull the bull a few feet away from the gut ball. He retied Patriot's lead rope and removed two meat sacks from the other saddle bag. Now, he could roll the bull onto its side and begin the tedious task of boning out the meat.

Forty-five minutes later, Buck moved one full meat sack to the side. He rolled the bull onto its other side to bone out the meat and fill the other sack. It always amazed him to see how much meat was on one of these huge animals.

Before loading the meat sacks into the pannier and heading up the slope, he decided to eat the sandwich he'd made before leaving the ranch house. He cleaned off his knife blade and bone saw with snow as best he could before putting them away. Buck then grabbed some snow and rubbed his hands together to wash off as much gore as he could. Wiping his hands on his pants, he retrieved the sandwich from his daypack strapped to the saddle horn, and took his first bite. Patriot brought her head around and sniffed. "Okay, I'll give you part of my apple when I get to it. Be patient."

As he ate the sandwich, he took in the snowy view of the valley below. Being out in nature by himself with his horse was definitely one of the hunting experiences he enjoyed most: the peacefulness, the smells, the rugged vastness, the whispers of the wind through the trees. When combined with the challenges of tracking an animal, field dressing and deboning the meat by himself, then leading his horse and bounty back to the ranch, he experienced a unique satisfaction that nothing else could equal.

After finishing his sandwich, he ate most of his Gala apple, then, as promised, gave the rest to Patriot. She wasted no time, chomping and swallowing what remained of the apple and its core. "Okay, Patriot, you ready for this?" He released her lead rope and tied it to a saddle ring; then taking her reins, led her over to the carcass. She sniffed loudly at the carcass, then, as her ears relaxed, raised her head. Buck positioned the orange pannier over the saddle horn and cantle; then lifted and placed one heavy meat sack into one pouch; then the other sack into the opposite pouch. Patriot shifted her feet a bit to adjust to the changing weight distributions. "Okay, steady while I cinch up the pouches."

Buck looked around to make sure he hadn't forgotten anything: hatchet, rope, his hunting knife, elk call, his hat, gloves, orange hunting vest. He checked to make sure his rifle was secure in the scabbard. "Okay, let's head for home," Buck said tugging on Patriot's reins. She hesitated slightly before taking her first step up the slope, as if anticipating how difficult it was going to be for her to carry this added weight uphill in the snow. "Once we get up to the road, it'll be a lot easier for you, Patriot."

The first 75 yards up the slope were uneventful, as the incline wasn't too steep. The next part of the slope grew steeper, however, and footing became more difficult. Buck's boots would slip occasionally, hindering his forward progress. The heavy weight on Patriot seemed to aid her traction for a time, as her hooves would penetrate the snow down into the dirt. But, about 150 yards up the slope, her right front hoof lost traction, and when she attempted to recover, her rear hooves began to slide backwards. Buck realized what was happening, and attempted to assist her by holding on to her reins. He was pretty confident she would recover like she always did, but she continued to slide backwards pulling Buck with her. She began to jerk her head in an attempt to keep her balance; her eyes grew large with fear. When Buck realized he was hindering her recovery by holding on to her reins, he let go of them. She could now control her head and stay upright, but she continued to slide backwards. Then, her rear legs slid into an obstruction—perhaps a rock or tree limb under the snow. The momentum and heavy weight caused her to rear, then flip over backwards and roll down the hill. Buck stared helplessly at her legs in the air, the meat sacks flying out of the pannier, tossing pieces of meat in every direction as they tumbled in the snow. She continued to roll until the short, bushy fir trees stopped her—just like they had the bull. Buck half-jogged and half-slid down the slope as fast as he could, expecting to see her stand up. But she didn't. On the way down, he passed pieces of elk meat, and his rifle now missing part of its stock.

When he reached Patriot, she was on her left side; a nasty, bleeding cut on her face. She was breathing but seemed to be dazed. Buck grabbed a handful of snow and placed it against the wound to help stop the bleeding. Seconds later, she seemed to regain consciousness, and moving her legs, positioned herself to stand up. Buck grabbed her reins to assist her and keep her from running away. When she managed to stand, her legs were wobbly and shaking uncontrollably.

"Easy, girl," he said rubbing her neck. "Just relax for a bit while I check you out." The saddle was askance and needed to be straightened. He loosened her cinch, adjusted the saddle and blanket then retightened the cinch. Fortunately, the saddle was intact and none of the straps were broken. He walked around her and didn't see any other severe wounds. He tied her lead rope to a nearby tree. "Just stay here while I gather things up," he said gentling stroking the side of her face. He retrieved the pannier that was now free of the meat sacks, the many chunks of meat that had been launched from the sacks, and his broken rifle. His scope wasn't broken, but he was sure it would need serious adjustment. He knocked the snow from the lenses and wiped them with his kerchief. He knew the stock would need to be replaced, so he didn't bother to look for the piece that had broken off.

Then, he returned to Patriot, who was still shaking. He released her lead rope and tied it to the saddle ring. Grabbing her reins, he attempted to lead her over to the gathered items. "Come on, Patriot; you're okay." But, she refused to walk. Buck hated to resort to a stick, but it always seemed to work on a stubborn or scared horse. He found a branch sticking out of the snow and snapped it off, making sure Patriot could see him holding it as he approached her. That did the trick. She followed him to the pannier and meat sacks that needed to be reloaded and secured. He kept the stick handy just in case he needed it again.

To help prevent Patriot from sliding backwards on the snow again, Buck removed the hatchet from the saddle bag. When they reached the steeper grade, he chopped through the snow to expose dirt that would give her more traction, until they reached the logging road above them. It was a tedious, slow process, but it worked.

When they stepped up onto the logging road, Buck patted her on the neck then rechecked the gear to make sure everything was secure. He checked her wound that had stopped bleeding. He talked with her and stroked her neck while she caught her breath and regained her confidence. When her legs were no longer shaking, he led her down the road toward home.

It was late afternoon by the time they descended the gulch leading down to the ranch. The snow was wetter at this elevation and every once in awhile, Patriot's hooves would launch a glob of snow forward hitting the back of Buck's boots. Buck grinned. "Payback for what I've put you through today?" He was spent and he was sure Patriot was as well, given the traumatic ordeal she'd been through, and her long trek back to the ranch carrying the heavy meat sacks.

Buck stopped at the garage to remove his rifle, the meat sacks and the pannier. Then he led Patriot over to the hitching post outside the corral across from the ranch house, where he removed the saddle and tack. Before releasing her into the corral, he grabbed some ointment from the tack house, rubbed some into her facial wound, and fed her some well-deserved grain. When she was done, Buck released her into the corral and gave her some hay and water. "You survived a tough afternoon, Patriot," Buck said patting her neck. "Rest well tonight," he added walking back toward the garage.

I'll take care of the meat tomorrow, Buck said to himself, placing the meat sacks on the cold cement floor of the detached garage, then closing the side door. Grabbing his broken rifle, he shuffled toward the back door of the ranch house. He removed his wet boots and socks in the utility room, then padded over to the wood stove to light a fire. *Dinner'll have to wait; I just need to sit a spell and rest my tired body....*

A Swifter, Kinder Death

The breeding adult male and female gray wolves led their pack members through the Western Montana snow. About six inches of new snow had fallen throughout the night, which made travel difficult and tiring. In about two hours, it would be getting light; the adults hoped to soon cross some fresh deer or elk tracks in the new snow. They could all sleep during the day—hopefully with full stomachs.

They'd found no tracks in the Moyle Gulch drainage area, so had headed northeast toward neighboring Grouse Gulch. Each time they stopped, they sniffed the air as they combed the lower drainage area leading into Grouse. But they found nothing. All pack members were panting loudly as they climbed out of Grouse Gulch near the south end of Bobcat Pass. There was a fairly level logging road that ran through the Pass, so once they reached it, they could travel much more efficiently through the snow.

Three miles below Bobcat Pass, Buck Wiley grabbed his rifle, day-pack and two game bags before turning out the interior lights of his ranch house, and heading out to the corral. He'd come out to the corral about an hour and a half earlier to feed and water his horse Indigo, a gray Missouri Foxtrotter. The fact that it had snowed in the night helped Buck deal with the frigid 22 degree air that made his breath visible. Fresh snow always made it easier to find game.

"How ya doin', Indigo? Ready for some huntin'?" Buck asked as he approached the corral. He set his gear on the bench under the covered slab between the tack house and corral, then grabbing a lead rope, attached it to Indigo's halter and moved him out of the corral to the slab. Putting some grain in a feed bowl, he placed it in front of Indigo, who eagerly began eating. Buck brushed the gelding's back and belly, then using a hoof pick, removed debris his hooves had picked up in the corral. Then Buck began saddling: first the blanket, then the saddle, the cinches, breastplate straps and crupper. After filling the saddlebags with extra ammo, the two meat sacks and some baling twine, he lashed an orange-colored pannier to the back of his saddle and tied his daypack to the right side of his saddle. He then commanded Indigo to put his head down, slid a bridle over his nose, gently secured the bit in his mouth, and positioned the crown over his ears before fastening the throat latch. The last thing Buck did before turning out the bright tack house spot lights, was to bolt a round into his 7mm. 08 and engage the safety. He then topped off the three shot magazine with another shell from his pants pocket. He'd now have four quick shots, if he needed them. "Okay, let's see if we can cut some tracks!" Buck said, slipping his rifle into the scabbard attached to the left side of the saddle.

Buck put on his gloves, secured the ear flaps of his insulated trapper's hat, and walked Indigo out the fenced gate leading into the corral area. He led him down the driveway and past the wood pile across from the garage, before placing the reins over Indigo's neck, preparing to mount. The trotter patiently waited while Buck mounted and settled into the saddle. He didn't move until he felt Buck's legs tighten around him signaling him to move forward.

In a short distance, Buck urged him left with his right knee, toward the gully that would take them up to the south end of his property. Buck usually had to keep a tight rein on Indigo, who, having just finished his oats, would want to trot up the trail, but this morning,

Indigo walked up the snow-covered trail mindful of the hidden, slippery rocks underneath. "Atta boy, just take your time; we have plenty of time before daylight."

When they reached the barb-wired gate at the south end of his property, Buck dismounted, released the wire loop holding the gate in place, led Indigo through, then refastened the gate. Before remounting, he tightened the saddle cinch, then urged Indigo up the trail that would take them past Medicine Hill and the steep climb to the north entrance of Bobcat Pass.

Even without snow on the ground, the steep trail up to Bobcat was hard work for Buck's horses; this morning's snow made it even more difficult. Buck stopped several times to let Indigo catch his breath. White steam rushed from his nostrils, rapidly at first, then gradually slowing. When Indigo's breathing approached normal, Buck would turn him back up the trail.

As the wolf pack reached the intersection of the two logging roads at the north entrance to Bobcat Pass, they found the two sets of tracks. They could tell from the smell that they were elk—one larger elk, a cow; the other, her calf. For a moment they excitedly sniffed the tracks with subdued yelps, analyzing their freshness and determining the direction they were heading—east toward Harvey Creek. The adults urged the pack on, as the scent was very fresh. They might be able to catch the elk before they headed down the steep grade into the Harvey Creek drainage area. In only about an hour, the rising sun would begin to lighten the eastern sky.

The cow and her calf were feeding on the western flank of a small hillside dotted with Ponderosa pines, just north of the parallel logging road. The snow wasn't as deep here due to the trees, so they didn't have to dig down as far to find nourishment. The mother wanted to eat what they could find here before daylight; then head for the steep grade leading down into Harvey Creek—less than a mile away. This east-facing slope would provide plenty of hidden benches where they could rest and see any threats coming toward them from below. It gave the mother comfort to see her calf moving the snow aside and eating as fast as it could. The little one had learned quickly.

The pursuing wolves were about 300 yards away when the cow caught their scent. She immediately barked and led her calf east at a brisk trot. She felt confident that if they could make it to the steep hillside, they could elude the pack.

The breeding male knew this area well, and was determined to stop the elk before they reached the hill's eastern slope. He pursued the now elongated tracks as fast as he could and knew he was gaining on the smaller set of tracks that were lagging behind its mother's. The cow knew she was close—only about 100 yards to the steep slope. But, when she heard her calf's frantic bawl, she quickly stopped and turned to confront their enemy. She saw the large wolf tearing into one of her calf's hind legs. When she charged, the male released the leg. The pack quickly separated and formed their instinctive positions surrounding both elk. One of the younger wolves now darted in from behind the cow, who was facing the majority of the pack, to grab onto the injured rear leg of the calf. When the mother turned to chase away this attacking wolf, another pack member tore into the bloody leg of the calf now separated from its mother. Each time the mother would charge to free her bleating calf, another pack member would dart in and grab a hind leg or quarter with its powerful jaws. This terrifying game repeated itself over and over. The desperate mother knew she couldn't hold them off for much longer. At one point, one of the pack members was able to grab the calf's throat and drag her a distance away from the protective mother. The cow furiously charged this wolf as quickly as she could to get closer to her calf.

About fifty minutes after leaving the ranch, Indigo, sweaty from the long, steady climb, stepped up onto the logging road that would take them to the north end of Bobcat Pass. Buck dismounted and checked the saddle cinch while Indigo's breathing slowed to normal. Buck knew daylight was about 20 minutes away, so after remounting, he urged Indigo into a trot up the road. The gelding obeyed immediately, as if eager to stretch his legs. Buck's experienced eyes scanned the road, the treed slope on his left, and the drainage area to his right looking for fresh tracks, movement, unusual color or silhouettes. Just as they approached the juncture of another logging road, Buck reined Indigo to a stop. There in the snow, he saw the fresh tracks. Two sets of elk tracks heading east, *and* several sets of wolf tracks pursuing them. He immediately commanded Indigo to follow them. Buck hated what the wolves had done to the deer and elk populations in this area over the past several years. It had gotten more and more difficult to find game; in fact, last hunting season was the first one ever, he'd finished empty-handed.

Sensing Buck's urgency, Indigo aggressively followed the tracks, first down the adjoining logging road, then up into the trees where they veered after a short distance.

It was now just light enough for Buck to witness the frantic scene about 100 yards east of him. His hunting instinct told him to shoot the cow. It could be the only elk he'd get a shot at this season based on last year's experience. But, his hatred for the wolves took over. He wasn't going to let this opportunity go. He brought Indigo to a halt, dismounted and removed the 7mm .08 from the scabbard. He took a knee, moved the safety forward with his thumb, and fired. One of the wolves yelped, and the entire pack quickly bolted north, leaving the tired cow and her injured calf momentarily bewildered. When the mother realized all the wolves had left, she barked and urged her limping calf eastward.

Buck loaded another bullet into the chamber and added one into the magazine from his shell holder before sliding the rifle back into the scabbard. He remounted and rode up to the battle site. The snow had been torn up down to the soil; dozens of tracks littered the ground. Two sets of elk tracks continued east; one of the smaller tracks left a drag mark in the snow along with frequent blood droplets.

"Looks like we arrived just in time," Buck said aloud, dismount-iing to get a closer look. All the wolf tracks headed north; a signifi-cant blood trail marked the route of the biggest tracks. *This one isn't going far,* Buck surmised, gazing north. He was very tempted to follow the wolf tracks to see if his hunch was right, but he didn't want to go another season without any elk meat in his freezer. He remounted and ordered Indigo to follow the elk tracks.

In a short distance, the tracks crossed the logging road that rimmed the western slope of the Harvey Creek drainage area, then headed down the steep, brushy hillside. Buck knew from years of hunting elk, that directly following their tracks would cause them to keep moving. Once they were confident they were no longer being fol-lowed, they would look for a densely covered bench to hide and rest. So, Buck looked for a place to tie Indigo up to a tree with the lead rope. He removed his orange hunting vest and put it over the saddle so another hunter wouldn't mistake his horse for an elk. He loosened the saddle cinch, then grabbed his rifle.

There wasn't much of a breeze, but he could tell that the snow that periodically fell from tree branches, was moving from north to south. So he walked south down the logging road, past the elks' tracks for a reasonable distance until he found what looked to be a game trail that was safe enough to venture down. He took his time, carefully digging the soles and heels of his boots into the hillside as he slowly descended the snowy slope. Every few steps, he would stop and listen. Nothing! Not a sound. *If the cow doesn't think she's being followed, she will stop to rest.*

When he'd descended about 100 yards down the slope, he saw a densely shrouded area about 75 yards to his left. *If I were an elk, that's where I'd hide.* He decided he'd head toward this spot to see if his instincts were correct. *Fortunately, the snow is dry and quiet,* he thought. He moved very slowly and deliberately, carefully avoiding any debris that would make a noise. After each measured step, he immediately looked toward the area he was approaching for any movement. He would pause for about 30 seconds between each step.

When he was about 40 yards away from the well-covered spot, he peered carefully into the brushy area through his rifle scope. It was then that he saw the movement—just a slight one. He stared at that spot, frozen in his tracks. Then, he saw it again, a slight movement. He'd seen this same movement many times when hunting— the quick flick of an ear intently listening for any strange sound. Looking through his scope, Buck could now see through the foliage, how the cow was standing. Yes, there it was, facing north, with its body slightly turned toward the right at an angle. Buck knew if he attempted to move another step closer, he would probably spook the alert cow; so he very slowly squared up his feet and shoulders, aimed at the right shoulder of the cow and squeezed the trigger. **BOOM!** The cow collapsed but was attempting to right herself. Buck quickly approached the shelter and when he could clearly see its head, fired again. **BOOM!** The shot, which normally would echo down the drainage area and off the surrounding hills, was quickly absorbed by the surrounding snow. The calf, which had been sleeping about 15 yards away behind a downed log, suddenly sprang up and faced Buck. It was shivering, no doubt from fear and possibly from its injuries. It seemed paralyzed, not sure of what to do. Buck stared at it with his rifle lowered. *Should I just let it go...? It will surely perish without its mother's protection, and if the wolves find it....* Buck raised his rifle and aimed at its chest. *Sorry, little one, but my rifle will give you a much swifter, kinder death.* **BOOM!** The calf collapsed right where it had been standing. Death was instant.

Buck's 7mm .08 slug had slammed into the left hip of the adult pack leader, causing him to yelp and collapse into the snow. His instincts quickly kicked in. He stood up and headed north leaving a trail of blood. His confused pack followed him. Every few steps, the leader would stop, lie down, reach back and lick at his wound. The pack would stop and attempt to comfort him by licking him, and encourage him onward with their whines. The sixth time he stopped, he lay down, licked at his wound several times, then lay flat in the snow too weak from loss of blood to proceed. Surrounded by his loyal pack, he took his last breath, dying with his eyes open. His mate tried to rouse him but after about twenty minutes, realized he was lifeless. During this time, the rest of the pack sniffed at him, nudging him, and even lay beside him attempting to comfort him. When they heard a distant rifle shot, the adult female rose to her feet and commanded them to follow her. She led them north for a ways, then veered back toward Bobcat Pass where they had first discovered the elks' tracks. Pack members would take shelter and rest among the craggy red rocks of the outcrop just west of the Pass. It was close to their male leader; they could easily return to visit him. They could also continue their pursuit of the elk tracks to see if the calf had succumbed to its wounds. If so, they could all put a little food in their stomachs.

Buck lowered his rifle, removed his gloves and placed one of the finger holes over the barrel to protect it from debris. Then he leaned the rifle against a tree close to the deceased cow. He removed his hunting jacket, hung it from a branch, and took the Buck knife from his pocket, to field dress the cow. He'd done this many times by himself over the years, so he completed the task efficiently. The steaming innards brought welcome warmth to his hands. After removing the cow's gut sac, he located a limb and broke off a piece long enough to prop the cavity open to cool the meat.

Then he turned to field dressing the calf. First, he moved his rifle closer to the calf's carcass. He'd heard stories of grizzlies coming toward gun shots to take advantage of easy game, so wanted to be prepared—just in case.

When he was done with the calf, he wiped his knife blade against a nearby limb to remove as much blood and fur as he could, then using some snow, washed the blood off his hands. Wiping them off on his Army surplus pants, he put on his coat and gloves to shut out the frigid air, grabbed his rifle, and headed back up the trail to fetch Indigo.

Indigo nickered when he heard Buck approach. "Did ya miss me, big fella?" Buck asked patting him on the neck. When he put his rifle into the scabbard, Buck noticed how torn up the snow was around the tree, and knew that Indigo must have been anxious about being left behind. Buck removed the orange hunting vest from the saddle and put it on so he'd be "legal."

"Hope you've had a chance to rest a bit 'cause you're about to work your ass off." He untied the trotter's lead rope and led him south on the road and down the steep trail to the dead elk.

It was slippery going for both of them, particularly Buck who lost his footing and fell several times walking back down the now-packed snow. Indigo, trained to walk behind Buck, quickly halted to avoid stepping on Buck. His weight allowed his hoofs to penetrate the snow into the soil, so his footing was surer than Buck's.

"Okay, here's where the going gets a bit dicey." He led Indigo left and through the thick brush and downed limbs that the elk had hidden behind. Foliage and dead protruding branches snapped as Indigo broke through the natural enclosure. He sniffed the air as if attempting to identify the unfamiliar but not totally foreign scent. This wasn't his first elk hunt with Buck, and he'd been trained to not spook when near dead animals. "Over here, boy," Buck urged tying the lead rope to a tree not far from the cow.

Buck made sure the saddle cinch was tight, then untied the orange pannier from the back of his saddle, unraveled it and placed it over the saddle horn and cantle. He then removed the two meat sacks from one of the saddle bags. He once again took off his gloves and jacket, fetched his knife and began the tedious task of removing the hide and deboning the meat on each side. One side of meat in one sack; the other in the second sack. Buck knew that Indigo could handle the few extra pounds of meat he'd remove from the calf, but he'd have to lead

Indigo all the way back to the ranch.

After loading both sides of the pannier with the two meat sacks and securing the cow's hide to the pannier, Buck cleaned up his knife and hands again, put on his jacket and gloves and looked for a route they could take back up to the road. He knew that the trail he'd come down was too direct and steep—he didn't want another "Patriot Disaster," with his horse tumbling down the hillside. So he looked for a possible exit route just north of the dense enclosure. While Indigo patiently waited, Buck bushwacked his way diagonally up the slope toward the road, removing downed limbs and large debris that might compromise Indigo's footing on the slippery ascent. Using his boots, he aggressively scuffed the snow to expose some soil. When he was confident, Indigo could handle the grade he'd cleared, Buck returned and began to lead Indigo up the make-shift trail to the road. Several times, he stopped to let Indigo rest, checking his legs for any uncontrollable shaking. He didn't want Indigo's legs to give out before reaching the road, like Patriot's had a few seasons back. Should Indigo take a tumble down this grade into the brush, Buck would be walking back to the ranch without his horse, rifle, saddle and tack, and with no elk meat. *One more attempt and we should be there.*

Buck breathed a huge sigh of relief when Indigo stepped up onto the logging road. He praised the gelding, patting him on the neck. "Good job, boy! You deserve some oats when we get back to the ranch."

Man, it feels good to stretch out my legs after all that bushwacking, Buck thought heading north on the logging road that would eventually take them back to the ranch. He could tell that Indigo felt the same relief given his renewed pace—and that Indigo knew he was heading home to hay and oats. Walking helped Buck stay warm, and the snowy scenes provided a beautiful and peaceful return. With the exception of their steps, all around them was a silence. Periodically, a tree limb would release the snow it had trapped, creating a gentle shower of white crystals. Buck always felt a healthy sense of accomplishment after a successful elk hunt, completing the hard work of field dressing the animal, skinning and boning out the animal, and heading back to the ranch with full meat sacks and the hide on his loyal, dependable friend.

An hour later, Buck and Indigo exited the trees and stopped at the garage, where Buck removed the two meat sacks, the hide, the pannier, his rifle and daypack. He then led Indigo through the gate and over to the corral to remove the bridle, saddle and blanket. He poured some grain into Indigo's bowl and let him finish it before releasing him out into the pasture.

"Get a good rest, boy; I'll be back in a couple of days and we'll go back and see if we can find that wolf."

After some lunch and a short nap, Buck retrieved two five gallon buckets from the garage, took them into the kitchen and lined them with white plastic bags. Before retrieving one of the meat sacks from the snow outside the garage, to begin the tedious task of cleaning up the meat for his favorite Missoula butcher, he tossed the soiled pannier into the washing machine and set the cycle.

Ninety minutes later, after he'd finished cleaning the meat in both game bags, he cinched up the liners, carried them out to his snow-covered car and put them in the trunk. Returning to the house, he removed the clean pannier from the washer and hung it in the mud room to dry. He loaded his soiled hunting clothes, set the cycle and headed for the shower. A hot, steamy shower was always so welcome after a long day of hunting and cleaning game: washing off the dried blood, removing the deep chill from his bones; letting the hot water sooth his tight muscles and clean the scrapes and cuts accumulated during the hunt.

After toweling off, Buck shaved, locked up the ranch house and headed back out to his car. Heading down the driveway, he looked to his right and spotted Indigo out in the east pasture with two other horses. As his car's heater warmed up the cold interior during the 40 mile drive to Missoula, he could tell he'd sleep well tonight.

The pack remained sullen and hungry during their short stay in Bobcat Pass. They walked about with their ears flat and tails low, missing their leader. Periodically, individuals would emit a low mourning-like howl, then lie down.

About three in the afternoon, the female leader roused the pack and led them east to where her mate lay. As they approached, a raven and two magpies ascended into a nearby tree. The birds had already eaten the male's eyes, leaving red cavities in his skull, and were working on other soft tissue parts. The wolves sniffed at the now cold, stiffened carcass, the darkened bloody gunshot wound and dried red eye sockets. Members nudged the male in hopes of arousing him; some emitting a low howl.

After about 15 minutes, the adult female signaled it was time to pursue the elk tracks that headed east toward Harvey Creek. She knew from the blood trail that the calf may not have traveled far— perhaps it had even succumbed to its injuries. When they came to the logging road, they spotted other tracks leading in several directions. They busily checked them out with their keen noses before zeroing in on the elk tracks. They headed down the steep slope and in short order could smell the dead elk. Quickly finding them, they tore into their remains, pulling away the pieces of meat left on both carcasses. Their perseverance had paid off—not just the calf but the cow!

When the meat and other soft tissues were eaten, they devoured many of the bones. After eating what they could, they cleaned themselves with their tongues, lay down and rested. Tonight, their bellies would not be empty, but tomorrow, when the sun rose, their undying hunger would drive them to a new hunt.

Importance of Knowing Your Rifle

It was just getting to be shooting light when our horses, breathing hard from the climb up the trail from the ranch, stepped onto the logging road, which would lead us toward a bald knob north of us. We made them walk slowly on the road while they recovered. They expelled plumes of steam from their nostrils with each breath. It reminded me of a fast idling car with dual exhausts warming up on a cold morning. It had snowed about three inches during the night and was now clear and very cold.

After walking about a quarter mile, we rode past an opening in the trees to our left, which gave us an unobstructed view of the knob's bald top. We both stopped our horses at the same time. A huge bull elk stood regally at the top checking out the valley below him. He looked majestic, statuesque, steam pouring out of his nostrils, then trailing off to his sides.

"He's got to be five or six points!" I exclaimed in awe.

"Look at that sight, Brady! Do you think your 7mm mag would be able to reach him? There's no way my 7mm .08 can from this distance."

"I don't think so, Buck" I replied, unsure. I hadn't taken any long distance shots after my new *Tekka T3* arrived in August, just two months ago, and this looked to be at least a 400 yard shot—*uphill*.

"Well, our only chance then is to ride as fast as we can up this road and then up the right flank of the hill to see if we can head him off. As soon as he sees us heading his way, he'll run back over the hill into the thick stuff."

We both admired the spectacular sight for a few more seconds, then Buck said, "Okay, ready...let's *go!*" His dapple gray horse, Ivan, bolted into a full run up the road, my sorrel, Sonny, following. I had seldom been on a horse running at this speed but I was amazed at how smooth this Missouri Foxtrotter was.

When we neared the top of the hill on the right flank, Buck yelled, "Quick, Brady, get off your horse and grab your rifle. Run up to the crest and see if you can catch him before he heads back into the trees." With my rifle in hand, I ran as fast as my cold, stiff legs would carry me up to the crest. At one point, I leapt over some coiled barbed wire sticking out of the snow. When I reached the top, I looked to my left where the big bull had been standing...he was gone.

"Shit!" I said aloud. I ran a bit farther until I saw his splayed tracks, which led northeast and down into the thick, dark forest. It was obvious he was running. I followed his tracks for a ways, hoping he just might have stopped to look back. But, he was long gone.

I'm sure Buck could tell what had happened by my slow pace back to him and the horses.

"You were right, Buck. When he saw us approaching, he headed for the thick stuff—I could tell from his tracks that he was running.

"Well, ya win some; ya lose some. As you get to know your rifle better, you may find it could've reached that far." He handed me Sonny's reins. "Let's head out and see what we can find...."

That magnificent bull would be the only elk I saw that season hunting with Buck, but the next day, while we were hunting south of the creek in Grouse Gulch, I was able to experience the incredible power of my new 7mm mag. I was in the lead following a narrow up and down trail that paralleled the creek below us. When I came over the top of a rise in the trail, I saw a large Mule doe standing about 30 yards ahead of me with her right shoulder exposed. When my 7mm mag roared, the incredible impact of the bullet caused the doe to jump straight up into the air and flip onto her back. "Whoa...did you see that, Buck!"

"At least you got a chance to shoot your new rifle this trip, Brady. There's no doubt about its power. As you get to know your rifle better, you may find it could've reached that bull we saw. Take some long shots each time you go to the range."

"I will," I replied, shutting the rear cargo door of my Subaru Outback. "Speaking of that bull, you should ride up there next time you hunt—early, while it's still dark. Pick a good spot to stay out of sight and see if that bull's there when it gets light."

"You know, I may just do that. Jamie has been buggin' me to take her elk hunting; that may be a good first elk hunt for her."

"Thanks for another fun hunting season, Buck," I said giving him a customary bear hug. "See ya next season...and let me know if you get that big fella."

"I will...have a safe drive back home."

The scene of the doe jumping into the air from my bullet's impact was one of several that I reflected on as I drove back home to Lynden, but the memory that dominated my mind was that of the majestic bull standing so regally at the top of the hill in the cold early morning light, steam pouring from his nostrils. *Maybe I should have taken that shot....*

The following Sunday morning about 7:30, our phone rang.

"Hey Brady, hope we didn't roust you out of bed, but...remember that big bull we saw on top of the hill behind Tully's ranch?"

"Yes...."

"Turns out, he was a big 5 point."

"*Was...?*"

"Yeah, Jamie and I rode up there before daylight, and she got him with one shot from the 7mm .08. Her first bull! Wanna congratulate her?"

The following August, September and October, after taking some shots at 100 yards from various positions at the rifle range, I made sure to walk my target down to the 200 yard berm and take a few long-range shots. By the time I left for Missoula in late October, I felt confident that my rifle could easily reach an elk or deer at that distance and probably, well beyond. It had amazing power and velocity. *Remember, while the target may look a long way off to my eyes, my scope will bring it up close and personal.*

"Where do you want to hunt tomorrow morning?" I asked Buck after we put our horses in the corral and gave them some hay.

"Well, I'd like to take you over toward Welch Gulch and McKnight Gulch, which are east of Harvey Creek. We'll ride up the road behind Tulley's place, skirt the south flank of that bald knob where we saw that big bull last year, then head down toward Harvey Creek."

"Sounds good, Buck."

I'd never hunted that area before, but I'd ridden with Buck down part of Harvey Creek several years ago after we finally found our way out of a God forsaken dry creek bed south of Grouse Gulch, that empties into Harvey during spring run offs. While riding north along Harvey, he showed me an old miner's cabin just above the creek, that had pretty much caved-in on itself over the years. Buck told me that the first time he discovered it years ago, he found some of the miner's skillets and silverware inside the cabin under some rubble. Parts of the wooden handles on the silverware were still intact.

"We'll head into Harvey kind of through the trees because I don't want the guy who manages the ranch we'll ride through, to see us."

"Who owns the ranch, Buck?"

"Evidently some rich guy from back east, who hardly ever stays there. He's missin' out because it's one of the most scenic spots in this valley. If it were for sale and Leah and I could afford to buy it, we would. You'll see what I mean when we ride through it on our way to Welch."

It was just beginning to get light when we reached the opening where we'd spotted the magnificent bull last year. There was no snow this year but the early morning air was clear and crisp. It was going to be a beautiful fall day. We reined in our horses and looked up at the bare hillside.

"Wish you would have taken that shot now, Brady?"

I got off my horse, grabbed my rifle and looked at the top of the knob through my scope. "Yes!" I replied returning my rifle to the scabbard. "I know now that my rifle could have reached him from here."

"Well, Jamie's sure grateful you didn't shoot," Buck replied with a grin, urging Ivan forward.

Instead of following the logging road to the right as we typically did when we took this route, we continued straight and rode down a steep hillside into a gully. It was thick with trees and brush because the spring runoff ran through it. I followed Buck closely because there was no obvious trail and I had no idea where we were heading.

After about 20 minutes of navigating our way around fallen trees and through thick brush, I could see an opening up ahead. Buck reined-in his horse and waited for me to ride up next to him. "Okay, Brady. When we get to that opening, we're going to high-tail it across the open field to a gate. I'll go first; just follow me. Your horse will probably start running when mine does, so hang on."

My gut was suddenly in knots. I wasn't used to riding a running horse and was worried I'd get bounced off, or that my horse would step in a hole while running full bore and plant me face first into the dirt. I didn't want to end up paralyzed like Christopher Reeve.

"Okay," I replied nervously. I'm sure Buck observed the worried look on my face. I followed him through some leafless deciduous trees along one of the fingers of Harvey Creek; then through the water a ways, to hide our tracks. When we emerged from these trees, Buck removed his hunting hat then put his boots to Ivan, who exploded into a full run heading toward the southeast corner of the open field, about 300 yards away. My horse, Sonny immediately responded running about twenty yards behind Ivan. When I felt my hat beginning to leave my head, I grabbed it with my left hand, and leaned back in the saddle to keep from getting pitched forward. I knew I'd have serious saddle sores to deal with after this ride was over but at least I was staying in the saddle.

When Buck reached the gate at the far end of the field, he stopped and waited for me to join him. "Good job, Brady! Now, follow in my tracks; I don't want any prints to show in the dirt." He rode his horse along the grassy edge of the muddy service road. After about 50 yards, Buck cut across the road and headed up a game trail that switched back and forth across a steep west-facing Welch Gulch slope, stopping at one point so we could rest our horses.

Shortly after we'd resumed riding up the slope, Buck suddenly stopped, and pumped his left hand up and down, signaling me to dismount. My horse was facing uphill on the slope, which made it difficult to dismount. I actually fell onto my back when I tried to reach the ground with my right foot. I quickly got up, removed my rifle and looked up the hill to where Buck was staring. A large five point Whitetail buck was standing perfectly still about 40 yards away looking directly at us. I flicked my safety off, aimed at his chest and fired. **BOOM!** The buck dropped immediately.

"Nice shot, Brady! Man, that's as big a Whitetail buck as I've ever seen in these parts. You got yourself a nice one! Go ahead and tag it, then we'll do a quick gut job and come back for him on our way out of Welch. I wanna get over to McKnight Gulch in case any elk are out feeding."

"Man, his antlers are so symmetrical, Buck. He's a beauty! Thank you for spotting him and giving me the shot!"

"You're welcome, B," he replied getting off his horse. "I'll give you a hand here so we can get going."

Before remounting, I looked about for a landmark so I could find my prize on the way out of Welch. It always amazed me how easily Buck could locate an animal we'd shot earlier in the day; I sometimes struggled doing so. *Okay, about twenty yards north of the trail, just before it bends to the south.*

After putting our jackets and gear on again, we remounted and continued riding up to the crest of the slope. "That's McKnight Gulch," Buck said as we looked down into an open, wide drainage area. The sun was high enough now to shine on the east facing slopes above the creek; the west facing slopes were still in shadow. "We'll head down to that logging road and ride up a ways; hopefully we'll spot some elk grazing on that sunny hillside."

We made our way down the slope and, at the bottom, looked for a safe place to merge onto the logging road that ran from west to east. Once on the road, Buck said, "Let's trot the horses for a bit up this road. Keep your eyes peeled for elk, Brady."

Trotting through the cold air caused my eyes to water; I blinked to clear them. In about three hundred yards, the road veered to the north. We saw him at the same time and reined-in. A lone, young bull was grazing on the east facing slope across the drainage. His light brown coat really stood out with the sun shinning on him. "He doesn't see us," Buck whispered. "Let's walk the horses up the road just a bit more—that'll give us a nice broadside shot."

When we gained an acceptable angle on the bull, we both dismounted and Buck took Ivan's reins. "Okay, Brady...grab your rifle; mine won't reach that far. It's probably about a 400 yard shot. Take a knee and aim right at the top of his shoulder. I'll tell you where your first shot hits and you can adjust."

"Okay," I nodded getting my rifle and trying to keep calm and confident. I took a knee and looked through my scope, which brought him into close focus. I put the crosshairs at the top of his shoulder and fired. The loud **BOOM** broke the stillness of the early morning and echoed off the hillsides and down through the gulch.

"Just a hair high," Buck coached. "You were right on but about two inches high."

I bolted another shell into the chamber and this time placed the cross hairs a few inches above the sweet spot behind his shoulder. He'd raised his head at the first shot but had begun to feed again. **BOOM...THWAP!** I knew I'd hit him when I heard that unmistakable sound. He began to slowly walk down the game trail he was on. **BOOM...THWAP!** He stopped and looked downhill.

"Shoot again, Brady!"

BOOM...THWAP! The young bull's knees buckled and he began to roll down the slope until his antlers tangled in a clump of dead tree branches.

"Nice shootin', Brady! You hit him three out of four shots at about 400 yards! That's some *fine shootin'!*"

"Thanks, Buck!" I replied excitedly with a big smile on my face. I grabbed his arm and giggled with excitement.

Buck smiled and said, "Reload and put your rifle in the scabbard; then let's lead the horses down this slope and cross over the creek to that hillside. When we get to him, I'll get a picture; then you can roll him down the rest of the way."

It was difficult to not hurry down the steep slope given how excited I was, but it was important to carefully navigate our way down and find a safe way to cross the stream bed. *Don't want an injury at this point,* I reminded myself.

"Okay, Brady. Give me your camera, grab your rifle and go stand by your elk." I couldn't help but beam with pride. It was by far the longest shot I'd ever made.

After Buck took a couple of pictures, I returned my rifle to the scabbard, then freeing the bull's horns from the debris, rolled him farther down the slope. Lead ropes in hand, Buck led our horses down the slope behind me. The bull got hung up a couple more times, but after I released him, he came to rest on his back, on a flat area at the bottom of the drainage, about ten yards from the creek.

"Could this be a more perfect place to dress him out!" I exclaimed removing my *Hoochie-mamma* cow call, orange hunting vest and wool jacket.

"It's definitely your morning, Brady," he replied tying our horses to nearby trees, and removing two meat sacks from my saddle bags.

"Being a young bull, his meat should be pretty tender, Buck. I think I'd like to get some steaks out of him."

"No problem. Instead of boning out the hind quarters, we'll remove them and carry both out in your pannier. I'll show you how to do that."

"Great!" I replied. Over all the years, I'd hunted with Buck, we'd always boned out the entire elk.

"We'll bone out just the front quarters and carry that meat and the back straps out in my pannier. With this weight distribution between us, we should be able to ride a good part of the way back to the ranch, but we'll have to walk them up and down any steep slopes."

"With the blessings I've been given this morning, I don't mind walking, Buck. It'll be well worth it."

After field dressing the bull, we severed the lower hind legs to minimize weight, then removed the hide on one side. After removing the back strap, Buck showed me how to cut around the hind quarter and release the socket so we could remove the entire hind quarter. We set it on one of the meat sacks while we removed the meat from the front quarter. After rolling the bull over, we repeated the same procedure on the other side.

When we'd finished both sides, we each lifted a hind quarter and simultaneously placed them into the pannier on my horse, legs facing backwards. We then cinched them down with the attached straps. Next, we hoisted the meat sacks of boned meat into the pannier on Buck's horse and strapped them down. Buck secured the rolled-up elk hide to the back of his saddle.

I found a small bar of soap in my daypack so we could wash our hands in the creek. "Pretty nice to be so close to a creek after field dressing," I said handing Buck the soap. "If the water weren't so damned cold, we could bathe before heading for the ranch," I chuckled. I looked at the sky as I wiped my hands on my pants. Gray clouds were beginning to roll in from the southwest, bringing with them a chilly breeze. I rolled down and buttoned the sleeves of my red and black flannel shirt. After putting on my hunting jacket, I took in the entire scene. It was one of those moments you want to capture in your memory forever, for you know you'll probably never experience it again. A rare moment in history, a rare moment in my life. I took a deep breath. *Thank you so much, Lord!*

"Thanks for bringing me over to this area this morning, Buck! What an incredible morning it's been!"

"Yeah, I'd say you've had a pretty productive morning, Brady," he smiled. "Let's go retrieve your buck."

After looking about to make sure we had all our gear, we grabbed our lead ropes and led our horses up the drainage until we found a game trail that would take us up to the logging road.

"I think I'll eat my sandwich as we ride back on the road," announced Buck unzipping his day pack. "Care to join me, Brady?!"

Before rounding the bend that would leave these unforgettable events behind us, I turned in my saddle for one last look. *So glad I practiced all those long shots at the range; I know now what my rifle can do.* I turned back around and took a bite of my peanut butter and jelly sandwich.

"Let's dismount and lead them up to the crest," Buck directed when we reached the east-facing slope that had led us into McKnight Gulch. We took our time, stopping a few times on the steep slope to rest the horses. When we reached the crest, we stopped to give the horses another rest and to pee. Now that we'd be heading downhill, we remounted and rode toward Welch Gulch.

"Think you can find your buck, Brady?"

"I think so," I replied following the tracks we'd made riding to McKnight Gulch. About halfway down the slope, I saw two magpies fly up and knew we were close to the gut pile and carcass. I didn't even have to follow the trail to where it turned south. We cut through the trees and there, about thirty yards ahead of us, was the carcass.

"Let me get a picture of you with your buck before we remove his hide, Brady. Stand over him and lift up his head. His coloring is really striking!" he added snapping a picture. "You know, he'd make a beautiful mount—do you want to do that or do you just want the horns?"

"Oh, man, that's so tempting, Buck...he is beautiful! But, we really don't have the kind of house for a head mount. And, I don't think Patsy would go for it.... However, I definitely want his antlers; they're so symmetrical."

While Buck boned out the second side, I used the bone saw to remove his antlers. I had to stop several times to blow on my hands in an attempt to warm them. "Man, that breeze is cold!" I declared. I glanced up at the sky. The steel-gray clouds had now shrouded the sun and signaled snow before long.

We added the boned venison to the two sacks carrying the boned elk meat, and after rolling up the buck's hide, placed it over the saddle in front of me before we began leading the horses down the west facing slope toward Harvey Creek. I turned and glanced back at the buck's remains. *Thank you,* I said paying a final, silent tribute. *And, thank you, Lord for this very special morning!*

I glanced at my watch as we neared Harvey. It was 2:55 and it looked and felt like it could start snowing any minute. I stepped in Buck's footsteps as we approached the gate to the pasture we'd sprinted across earlier this morning. I could see a light on in the ranch house at the far north end of the pasture.

"Let's walk along the trees as long as we can, then we'll mount up and cross the creek so we don't get our feet wet," explained Buck. "I think it's late enough and gray enough that we won't stand out, and it looks like the manager's in his house."

As we approached Harvey Creek, a strong spiritual experience came over me. We were enshrouded by a purple aura—the color the sky gets right before it snows. The open, quiet pasture was bordered by leafless deciduous trees. Buck was riding ahead of me, Ivan carrying a full pannier and elk hide, his steamy breath carried away by the chilly breeze now out of the north. The Whitetail's hide rolled up across my saddle horn helped warm my fingers that I'd tucked underneath it. The burbling creek muffled the sound of our horses' hooves as they walked through the rocky creek bed.

Right before we reached the trees on the other side of the creek where we'd head for the gulley and back up to the logging road behind Tully's ranch, I saw a snowflake lazily float down before me. I watched another land on the hide in front of me. "It's starting to snow, Buck."

"Perfect timing!" he responded. "The snow will cover our tracks."

The next leg of our return trip to the ranch was the toughest, as we led our horses up through the thick brush and around fallen trees in the gully, working our way toward the logging road. But, I didn't mind. I was bringing back full sacks of elk meat and venison, a beautiful set of Whitetail antlers, and treasured, unforgettable memories.

Once at the top, it was an easy walk down the logging road that led back to Buck's ranch. Snowflakes swirled about us now leaving a light skiff on the road. By the time we left the road and began the final leg back down the trail to the ranch through the trees, we were surrounded by wintry scenes. The steady, delicate snowfall created a peaceful silence, interrupted only by the sounds of our horses and the leather tack and gear they secured. By now, my legs felt heavy from all the walking over the course of the day, but Sonny, who knew he was close to home and some hard-earned grain, had to be reminded from time to time to walk behind me on the trail.

Tomorrow, after cleaning up the meat, Buck and I would say our good-byes, then I'd begin the long drive back to Washington State. I knew I'd be tired from three days of hunting, but I'd be riding a wave of indelible memories.

Majestic Buck
In Bobcat Pass

Buck reined Jewell to a stop and eyed the tracks in the snow.
"Can you tell what kind of tracks they are?" I asked from my
saddle.

"Wolf tracks. Climb on down, Brady and I'll show you...." He
squatted down pointing to the tight formation of tracks on the game
trail that cut across the slope we were on. "See the nail impressions
along with the pad prints?"

"Yes."

"Well, you'd just see the pad prints, if it were a cougar or a bobcat.
And, see how close the tracks are together...the pack is just walking
together here, no doubt looking for their next kill. Want to follow
them a ways?"

"Sure," I replied, curious to see where they might lead us.

Leading our horses on foot, we followed the close-knit tracks for
about a half mile, until the prints broke ranks and fanned out from
one another—as if checking something out. Sure enough, a short distance away, we saw the tracks of a deer heading down slope. I could
just envision the now excited wolves, sniffing the deer's tracks, then
the air before running down the slope in pursuit.

"Probably a doe judging from the size of the tracks," Buck said.

"Should we follow them?"

"No, the chase could go on for miles through God-only-knows what terrain before they finally bring it down."

We stood there for a few minutes eyeing the tracks. I wondered when the deer would realize it was being pursued by wolves; how far it would get before being caught; its fear...its futile struggle.

"If wolf-lovers could witness a wolf kill, they wouldn't be so sympathetic to them," Buck said lifting the reins over Jewell's neck to remount. "When the wolves eventually tire or trap the deer, they bite the deer's hamstrings so it can't run anymore. When the deer goes down, they begin eating it—while it's still alive."

I winced. "Oh, my God, what a painful, terrifying death that must be."

"Yep; that's why if I see a wolf, I'm going to shoot it," Buck said checking his cinch.

"Well, let's saddle up, B; by the time we get back to camp, it'll be getting dark."

In past years when I hunted with Buck in the snow, the ground looked like a freeway interchange with all the deer tracks crisscrossing in this area. But, this year, deer tracks were very few and far between.

Our current elk camp was an old trapper's cabin that we "inherited" from another hunting party. Two years ago, for reasons unknown to us, they had decided to abandon it as a hunting camp. Perhaps one of the elder family members had fallen ill and could no longer make the rugged trip back into Moyle Gulch to maintain it, or perhaps they had decided to trade the cold hunting seasons for warmer climates.

In June, Buck and I had packed some equipment in to this camp, from our previous camp in Grouse Gulch, after a vindictive DNR agent had dismantled it with a chain saw. The day we brought the camp equipment to the now-abandoned trapper's cabin, Buck cut down a few trees to buck up for fire wood we'd need come hunting season. One of the lodgepoles fell into a copse of trees and brought down with it, a plastic garbage can full of camp supplies: silverware, plastic plates, coffee pot, lanterns, etc. The previous users of this camp had hoisted this cache into the grove of trees, no doubt hoping to return some season to re-establish their camp. Had the lodgepole not fallen into this grouping of trees, we would probably never have discovered this cache. It was very well-hidden.

Over the course of the summer, Buck and his sons had made several trips back to repair some of the roof's lodgepoles, assemble the camp stove and its chimney, set up the kitchen utensils, bunk supports, and erect two horse corrals.

"Man, that stove is going to feel mighty good," I said as we rode down toward the nearly hidden trapper's cabin. The trapper had erected his small log cabin down in a hollow, where an underground spring bubbled up just outside its west wall. But, its sheltered location felt a few degrees colder than the trail not far above it.

We tied our horses to a hitching post Buck had installed near the east side of the cabin to unload our rifles, day packs and some of the items in our saddle bags. We then led the horses one by one to the back of the cabin where we unsaddled them, placing the saddles and blankets on a makeshift saddle stand under the overhang of the roofing tarp.

"Make sure the stirrups and cinches are off the ground, Brady; we don't want any mice chewin' on 'em." We placed the saddle blankets on top of the saddles upside down so they'd dry out a bit; then covered the works with a separate plastic tarp.

After leading the horses into the corral and securing its sliding gate, Buck filled two pans with feed for them, and I filled two water buckets from the underground spring.

"Now we can get a fire goin', B," Buck said lighting one of the propane lanterns inside the small dark interior. "Go ahead and use some of that kindling and logs to get our stove goin'," he said nodding to the pile of kindling and cut logs in the corner by the stove. "No flares this year—my railroad connection retired, but this gel stuff works pretty well. Just squeeze some of it on the kindling."

When the stove began to heat up the small interior, we removed our jackets and hung them on nails Buck had driven part way into a cross pole over the bunks.

"You guys sure did a nice job fixin' up this place," I said checking out the pots and pans hanging from their individual nails on the kitchen side. Below them, the silverware and knives rested in an organizer; the plastic dishwashing tub, dish soap and hand soap were to the right; the towels and washcloths hung at the north end of the kitchen counter.

"Thanks—we did put in a few hours back here. This is the real deal, huh!—staying in the same cabin a trapper used over 100 years ago."

"Sure is," I replied wondering if the trapper had organized his interior much the same. *Kitchen may well have been on same side—given the location of underground spring...stove could well have been in the same place—just inside the door close to the wood and on the kitchen side. He wouldn't have had a plastic tub for washing dishes or any liquid dishwashing soap...but he probably had a root cellar—perhaps in the center of the floor covered by something.... He no doubt kept his rifle handy...just in case an unwanted visitor showed up....*

We filled several pans with water from the spring to boil for food, and for washing up the dishes after our dinner of canned ravioli.

"Think the trapper who lived here ever had to confront bears and wolves?" I asked stoking the stove.

"No doubt. Can you imagine how far the smell of cooking food would travel back here!? Would have been hard for critters to resist," Buck said opening a can of ravioli.

"Maybe that's how he got some of his pelts.... Can you imagine how long the winters would be back here!?"

"And how much wood you'd have to cut each summer for survival! You know what they say, B...better him than us."

We ate our gourmet dinner of ravioli sitting on two cut logs that served as seats; then washed up our bowls, pans and spoons. We made sure the horses had water and were secure; brushed our teeth, peed, put a couple more logs on the fire, turned off the lantern, and slid into our sleeping bags. I made sure my headlamp was handy in case I had to get up in the night, and checked to make sure my bear spray was within easy reach—just in case.

Not long after we'd both fallen asleep, we were jolted awake by a loud shriek from one of the horses.

"Do you think they smell a bear, Buck?"

"Naw—the older horse is pickin' on the younger one. Dawgone! I'll have to move the younger one up to the other corral; otherwise we'll be hearing that all night. If you wouldn't mind lighting the lantern and holding it for me, I'll grab a halter and move him."

"No problem," I replied turning on my headlamp. I slipped into my camp tennis shoes, found the matches and lit the lantern hanging from a crossbeam on the kitchen side. I put on my hunting jacket before leading us out the door toward the corral.

"What's goin' on out here?" Buck asked releasing the chain holding the corral gate closed. He isolated my smaller, younger horse, Sonny, put the halter on her and led her out the gate toward the smaller corral. "Mind closing up that gate again, Brady?"

I had to chuckle as I watched Buck wearing only his moccasins, lead Sonny up to the other corral.

"There, that should solve that problem," he commented shuffling back toward the cabin. Before we re-entered the door, Buck said, "Turn off the lantern for a sec, B. Look up at those stars...."

The night sky above us was an infinite collection of dazzling stars.

"Oh, my God! I haven't seen stars like that since I was a young boy growing up in Omak. Sure don't see this where we live now."

After slipping back into our sleeping bags, Buck said, "You asked about a bear earlier...did I tell you about the dead black bear I found this summer over in the Tyler Creek area?"

"No," I replied eager to hear the story.

"Well, I was riding up Tyler Creek, not far from where we took the kids fishing years ago, when I saw this dead black bear. When I rode up to get a closer look, I saw a big pile of bear shit—much bigger than typical black bear scat. And, then I saw the footprints. Brady...they were *grizzly* prints!"

"Do you think the grizzly killed the back bear?"

"Oh yeah. That's what happens when a grizzly comes into a new area. The black bears either leave or the grizzly will kill them."

"Oh, my gosh. So, there's a grizzly back in this area?"

"At least *two*. When I called the fish and game department to report what I'd found, they told me they're aware of at least two of them back in here, and, the guy I spoke with warned me to be careful because one of them is a big male. On that note, Brady...sleep tight and don't let the grizzly bears bite."

"Night, Buck...." I reached out to make sure my bear spray was still within easy reach before snuggling down into my bag.

After getting a fire going the next morning to warm up the now frigid cabin, we gave the horses some feed and water, put on some water to boil, and started breakfast.

"While I'm cookin' up the hash browns, would you mind deflating our pads and putting our sleeping bags in their stuff sacks, B? No use stayin' back here another night 'cause there isn't any game around here—thanks to the damned wolves."

"Where do you want to hunt today?"

"Well, I think when we get to Moyle Saddle, we'll head down toward Grouse to check out that area; then ride back up to Bobcat Pass before headin' back to the ranch. Maybe, *if* there's still a deer alive in these parts, we'll cross paths with it."

By the time we closed up the cabin and saddled up, the sky was beginning to lighten.

"Looks like it's going to be a beautiful, clear day, Buck."

"Yeah, especially if we kill somethin', B."

Our ride on the trail out of Moyle toward Grouse proved uneventful—no fresh sign of deer or elk.

"Damnable wolves!" Buck lamented as we rested our horses in Moyle Saddle. He panned the surroundings. "Did I ever tell you about the time I came upon a mountain lion and her cubs in this area?"

"No!" I replied listening with interest.

"You know that rocky ridge we ride across before heading down to the game trail that goes into Moyle?"

"Yes."

"Well, one year I was riding back to Moyle in about eight inches of snow, and just as I got to that rocky ridge, I saw a mountain lion and her three cubs eating on a deer she'd brought down. She screamed and hissed at me as soon as she saw me. One cub took off up over the ridge and the two others quickly followed. She kept glaring at me and growling until the last cub was out of sight. Slowly, she slinked away from the deer, looking back at me every few steps to make sure I wasn't pursuing them, then quickly disappeared over the ridge. In all the years, I've hunted back here, it's probably one of the coolest scenes I've ever witnessed. The next day, when I was hunting back here, I returned and saw them eating on the deer again."

"Oh, my gosh, Buck, that's incredible! Wish I'd been with you to see that!"

"Well, let's hope we see *somethin'* down in Grouse, B." He urged his horse to the right down a game trail through the trees. This trail bypassed the craggy ridges we usually rode across when heading into Moyle from Bobcat Pass.

A couple different times, Buck headed off this main game trail and zig-zagged his horse directly down the steep face until he came to lower, more secluded trails that paralleled the main game trail above us. We wove our way north walking around trees that had fallen in recent years, and now blocked previously established game trails. Eventually, we came to a small clearing where the morning sun lit up two immense, Ponderosa pine trunks. The deep contrast of their orange and black-veined bark was more vivid than any I'd ever seen. We stopped long enough to take our pictures beside them. It just seemed like the perfect morning to see an elk or deer—the crisp morning air, the bright sunshine exposing the depth of the forest. But, nothing!

After we'd ridden about another half hour, Buck veered left on a game trail that headed back uphill toward Bobcat Pass. The forest thinned as our horses climbed toward an area that had been logged several years back. Its undergrowth, exposed to the morning sunshine, displayed vivid autumn reds and oranges. *Okay, we're going to see something now,* I said to myself trying to keep optimistic and alert.

About halfway up the open slope, just below the pass, I saw Buck stand up in his stirrups as if he'd spotted something. He stopped and waved me up next to him. "I think I caught a glimpse of a buck up ahead, Brady," he whispered. "Get off your horse, grab your rifle and walk up ahead. If he's still there, you should spot him when you get just over that rise. Hand me your reins."

I grabbed my rifle and walked hunched over and as quickly and quietly as possible, heading for the rise. As I reached the crest, I slowly stood tall, and that's when I saw him—about 75 yards from me. He was the most magnificent Mule buck I'd ever seen: big, muscular, head held high, proudly displaying his impressive rack, strutting across the open slope from my right, steam flowing from his nostrils in the chill of the clear early morning air. I released the safety of my 7 mm mag, put the crosshairs behind his left shoulder and fired. **BOOM!** He collapsed immediately. I lowered my rifle and jogged toward him, shaking from adrenalin and excitement.

Buck came riding up to me with my horse in tow. "Nice shootin',

Brady! Wow, he's a *big* fella! They don't come much bigger than that around these parts," he said, riding over to his right to tie up the horses.

"Oh, my God, Buck. He was *sooo* majestic strutting across this slope," I said still shaking. "Thank you so much for spotting him, and letting me take him."

"You're welcome, B. Well...guess we'd better tend to him."

I don't know why I didn't take a picture of him with my disposable camera before we began field dressing him. Perhaps I was still in a state of excitement and awe; perhaps I wanted to finish quickly so Buck could find a deer or elk. But, to this day, I regret not taking a picture of him. Big, muscular body, five points on each side of his tall, thick, almost perfectly symmetrical antlers! *No wonder he's survived the wolves around here,* I thought while field dressing him. A part of me felt badly about shooting him, but then I thought, *maybe I did you a favor, big fella. It would just be a matter of time before the wolves would get you. An injury, an illness, old age, getting trapped—at some point they'd get the best of you. This morning, you died quickly, proud and in your glory.*

After boning out the meat and removing his impressive antlers, I tied a loop knot around the top of the plump meat sack and hefted it up around my saddle horn, where it hung down on the right side of my saddle. I proudly carried the antlers while we rode toward the logging road that cut through rugged Bobcat Pass.

When we got to where two logging roads converged, Buck headed up a slope and into the trees. "Let's cut through here, we just may jump something back in here."

"If we do, you take the shot, Buck. I'm perfectly satisfied with this treasure."

We rode up through the trees for about half a mile, then cut left down into a thickly treed area. In a short distance, I spotted a hunter in an orange vest standing next to a tree and nodded at him. He stepped out from behind the tree and put his hand up like he wanted us to stop.

"Must've been the shot we heard about 45 minutes ago."

"Probably so," I replied.

"Mind holdin' up that rack for a sec?" By this time, his hunting partner began walking over from his stand about 75 yards away to our right. "Yup...willin' to bet that's the big buck we spotted last year when we were hunting back here. I caught a glimpse of him running through the pass—like he was being chased by something."

"Probably wolves," Buck said. "Given the looks of things back in here, he's the only critter to survive them. Used to be deer and elk tracks all over the place back here."

I could tell from their postures this wasn't the news they wanted to hear. The hunter, who'd waved at me to stop, reached down to grab his freighter frame, then looked at his partner. "We might as well start walking down—there won't be another deer coming through here any time soon now." His partner nodded and headed back to his stand to retrieve his gear. "Tell you the truth...wish I were the one holdin' those horns, but congratulations to you." He put his arms through his pack frame. "That's an impressive rack!"

"Thanks. Hope you guys see somethin' on the way down," I offered as we urged our horses forward. As we rode out of the woods and down toward the logging road, I tried to estimate what time those guys had to get up this morning to walk all the way up here from the gate at Mullen Road by Tyler Creek. *It had to be about a three hour uphill hike carrying all their gear and rifles.... Hunters can't use motorized vehicles to get back here.* I felt so privileged to be able to hunt with Buck on horseback! *What a unique privilege and advantage!* "Thanks for this great hunt, Buck!" He glanced back at me, gave me a thumbs up and smiled. I looked at the impressive antlers I was carrying and grinned. *What a classic, memorable hunt this was—and on such a beautiful morning! Thank you, Lord!*

Scavenger

B uck Wiley shifted in the driver's seat and rolled his neck from side to side in an attempt to shed some of the tension from the long drive, and to encourage alertness for the rest of the drive to Missoula. He glanced over at the time on the dashboard: *about 9:30 Montana time.* It had been dark now for about three hours. Buck never looked forward to this long, curvy drive to and from his wife Leah's hometown of Clarkston, Washington where her parents still lived. During daylight, the beautiful scenery along the Clearwater River on Highway 12 helped distract him from the long drive, but after dark, the drive seemed endless. Both Leah and their three year old daughter, Jamie were asleep, slumped in their seats.

Driving north on Reserve Street, Buck nudged Leah, who was propped against her door frame. "We're just about home, Honey."

Leah stirred, her eyes squinted under the glare of the Reserve street lights. "Oh, my gosh...how long did I sleep?" she asked yawning.

"Oh, about two hours. Jamie's still asleep in the backseat," Buck said now heading north on Grant Creek Road, a dark, rural road northwest of Missoula. Buck had engaged the high beams to light up the two lane road that wove north.

As they neared the turnoff to their house, Leah reached back and gently patted Jamie.

"Time to wake up, Hon, we're just about home."

Jamie moved in her safety seat, briefly opened her eyes, then closed them attempting to resume her slumber.

The headlights lit up the entrance to the steep graveled driveway, which led up to their two story house nestled into the hillside, surrounded by Ponderosa pines. As the car reached the top of the leveled driveway pad, the headlights revealed the overturned garbage can and its contents strewn about the area.

"Oh, my gosh, Buck! What a mess!" Buck stopped the car for a minute and they both surveyed the alarming scene.

"Gotta be a bear to make a mess like that," Buck said quietly, not wanting to alarm Jamie. "Darn! That's all we need this time of night. I'll take care of it while you put Jamie to bed," he added pulling the car into the carport next to his pickup.

"Thanks! I'll turn on the spot lights so you can see."

Tired from the long drive, Buck was looking forward to hitting the sack, as he had to teach the next day. *Darn the luck,* he thought rounding up the scattered debris and tossing it back into the garbage can. He returned the can to its built-in storage space in the car port and put the lid back on. For good measure, he lifted the heavy chopping block from outside the carport, and placed it on the lid's top. *Hopefully that will discourage the bear for now.*

"Still think it was a bear?" Leah asked, as Buck walked into their upstairs bedroom carrying their suitcases.

"Pretty sure. It would take an animal with a lot of strength to get that can out of its framed-in structure, and to remove the lid. And, the plastic bags weren't just ripped, like a raccoon might do; they were all torn apart."

"It makes me pretty nervous to think a bear is bold enough to come into our yard and help himself. What if Jamie or I were outside when it approached?"

"I'll check it out more closely tomorrow," Buck replied attempting to allay her fears, "but right now, I just want to get some sleep. Five thirty's going to come early."

"Might want to keep Jamie inside today, Leah," Buck said before heading out to his truck for work. "Just in case it was a bear, that might return for more grub. It's still too dark out there to see any tracks; I'll check things out more when I get home this afternoon." He kissed her, then headed for the door. "Oh, remember—shot gun's in the closet across from the laundry room—just in case," he added.

"Yeah, right," Leah replied sarcastically. "And, you expect me to use it!?"

As Buck opened the door to his classroom at Sentinel H.S. in Missoula, Russ Peters, whose classroom was next door, approached. "How was your trip to Clarkston?"

"Okay. We had a good visit with Leah's folks and caught up with some of the local news, but man, that is a *looong* drive! It's so curvy and *slow*. Oh, and get this. when we got home, we discovered garbage all over our driveway. It had to be a bear to drag our almost full garbage can out of its storage frame, remove the lid and scatter garbage like that."

"Oh, shit. You know what that means...it'll be back. You may want to call Fish and Game."

"Or just shoot it," Buck quickly added, just as the bell for first period rang. "I sure don't want it comin' around with as much as Leah and Jamie like being outside. Leah's pretty worried right now."

"I can understand—keep me posted," Russ said heading for his classroom.

"Mommy, can we play outside after breakfast?" Jamie asked maneuvering her little spoon to scoop some more Cheerios out of her cereal bowl.

"Well, maybe later," Leah replied looking out the kitchen window in front of the sink. "I was thinking about making some chocolate chip cookies after breakfast. Would you like to help me?" She hoped such a project would distract Jamie from going outside.

"Yes!" Jamie replied eagerly banging her spoon on the table.

"Okay. Finish your breakfast; then we'll get started." Leah removed the cookie recipe from her recipe box and began to gather and measure out the ingredients. She found herself frequently looking out the kitchen windows, panning the visible landscapes to make sure the bear hadn't returned. Earlier that morning before Jamie awoke, she had checked the closet across from the laundry room to make sure she knew the exact location of the shotgun. Above it, on the shelf was a box of 12 gauge shotgun slugs. She'd watched Buck load and shoot the shotgun before, but she'd never had any desire to fire it herself. It made such a loud roar and she could tell that it kicked like hell. But... she'd do what she had to do, if it came to that.

"Ready to help me make the cookies now?" Leah asked after wiping Jamie's face and hands with a warm wash cloth.

"Yes!" she said jumping up and down.

Leah tied a dish towel around Jamie's waist. "There—now you have an apron just like Mommie." After sliding a kitchen chair over to the counter, Leah lifted Jamie up. "Okay, put this cube of butter into the mixing bowl; now pour in this white sugar... now the brown sugar.... Good, now watch Mommie mix them together.

"Let's sing the alphabet song while I run the mixer.... Ready...A,B,C,D...E,F,G....

"Okay, now add this egg." Leah provided an extra hand while Jamie lifted the bowl containing the egg and slid it into the mix. "Now, this little bit of vanilla....

"Okay, now let's dump in these chocolate chips!"

"Can I have one, Mommie?"

"Yes, but just one, we need the rest for the cookies."

Jamie happily put the chip into her mouth and watched while her mom added the chips and completed the mixing.

"Okay, we're ready to put the cookie dough on these sheets so they can go into the oven.... Here, you can lick one of these beaters while

I make this batter into little balls and put them on the sheet, okay?"

Jamie was too busy attacking the beater with her tongue to respond.

After placing the baking sheets in the oven, Leah began to clean up the bowls and utensils in the kitchen sink. As she did so, she frequently looked out the sink window.

When the oven timer beeped, Leah checked the tops of the cookies with her finger. "One more minute," she said. She didn't mind the delay, as she knew it was going to be a long day, staying inside until Buck arrived from work.

"Okay, cookies are done! But, we'll have to wait just a few minutes until they cool off."

"Then can we go outside, Mommie?"

"We'll see," Leah said wiping the batter from Jamie's face and hands. "Want me to read you a story while we wait for the cookies to cool?"

"Okay," Jamie replied running to the book basket in the living room. "How about this one?" she asked excitedly handing it to her mom.

"*Goldilocks And The Three Bears*...ahh...sure.... Let's go sit on the couch in the living room."

Jamie nestled next to her as she began the story, "Once upon a time...."

After finishing the story, Leah glanced up at the clock above the wood burning stove: *only 10:45! Wish it was 1:45.* "Okay, let's go see if the cookies are cool enough to eat," she said, getting up from the couch and heading for the kitchen. She placed one of the cookies on a napkin on the kitchen table, and Jamie climbed up on her chair to enjoy it.

Leah didn't normally let Jamie watch cartoons during the day, but today, Leah needed help. After Jamie washed down her second cookie with a small glass of cold milk, Leah asked, "Want to watch cartoons for awhile, until lunch time?"

"Yes!"

Leah finished cleaning up the kitchen and planned out dinner while Jamie sat on the living room floor staring at the TV. Leah was relieved when the hour and minute hands on the kitchen clock both pointed upwards. She knew that after lunch, Jamie would go down for her nap for at least an hour—maybe more.

While Jamie napped, Leah did a few inside chores, looking out various windows to make sure the scavenger hadn't returned. By the time she'd prepared a few items for dinner, it was 2:00 and the tension she'd felt throughout the day began lifting a bit. Today, she was going to let Jamie sleep as long as possible. Buck could play with her in the yard after dinner, until Jamie was worn out and ready for bed.

Jamie was up at 2:30 and asking to go outside. At 3:30, when Buck's truck labored up the driveway and parked next to the carport, Leah felt a huge relief.

"*Daddy!*" Jamie shouted when Buck entered the door.

Buck swept her up in his arms and kissed her, making her giggle.

"Mom and I baked cookies today!"

"You did...can I have one!?"

"Sure!" she responded squiggling out of his arms and running into the kitchen.

"Any sign of the bear today?" Buck asked Leah quietly when Jamie was out of earshot.

"No, thank God. But, we're *really* ready to go outside for a bit," she added rolling her eyes.

Buck could tell it had been a long day for Leah. "Not a problem, let's go...it's a beautiful day out there."

Buck chased Jamie about the yard, making her squeal when he caught her and lifted her in the air. He then pushed her on the tire swing. When Jamie'd had enough swinging, and wanted to be with Leah, Buck scoped out the driveway landing, looking for any tell-tale signs of a bear. It wasn't until he walked over to the east edge of the driveway, that he saw a definite pad print—a black bear's. *Next time it visits, it's dead,* Buck told himself.

After dinner, Buck walked down the driveway and one block over, to his closest neighbor, Tom Strand. Tom was in his back yard, chopping some wood for his wood stove.

"Hey, Buck, what's up?"

"Well, I came over to tell you that sometime over the weekend, while we were in Clarkston, a bear got into our garbage can and made quite a mess. Has that ever happened at your place?"

"No, but if it's been at your place, it's just a matter of time before it hits ours. What are your plans?"

"Well, if it comes back and I'm around, I'm going to shoot it. Can't have it comin' around the house and yard. Leah and Jamie love to be outside during the day—it's just too risky."

"I agree. Guess I'd better keep my rifle handy in case it comes our way; I'll let you know if it does."

"Thanks, Tom. Just wanted to let you know so, if you or your wife hear a shot, you'll know the reason."

"I'll let her know, Buck."

Before, turning in for the night, Buck loaded three slugs into his 12 gauge shot gun, engaged the safety, returned it to the closet, and shut the folding door.

For the next two days, there was no sign of a bear, and no issues with their garbage can. Then, on Thursday morning, a little after 2:00 am, Leah shook Buck out of a deep sleep. "Buck, the bear's back... listen!"

His heart racing, Buck sat up and tried his best to wake up. He didn't hear anything for several seconds, then heard the garbage can moving on the graveled driveway. He got up, found his moccasins, threw a lined flannel shirt over his bare torso, walked swiftly downstairs, grabbed the shot gun from the closet, and turned on the spots before heading out the door toward the driveway. With the sound of the door opening, the bear turned its attention from the open garbage can, to Buck, then ran toward the east side of the driveway.

Buck raised the shotgun and released the safety, but before he could shoot, the bear scrambled up a nearby Ponderosa pine. Buck could hear it climbing up the tree against the bark, but couldn't see it because the spotlights lit up just the driveway. He went back into the house, grabbed a flashlight, turned off the spots, and walked over to the tree the bear had climbed. Holding the flashlight in his left hand, he shined the beam up into the tree until he could see the bear's beady eyes looking down at him. Raising the shotgun with his right arm, he placed it against his shoulder and fired. **BOOM!** Almost immediately, there was a loud *wumph*, as the bear fell to the ground. Buck quickly ejected the spent casing and pumped another shell into the chamber. He held the beam on the downed bear, as he clutched the shotgun to his shoulder. Just as he was going to fire, the bear sprung to its feet and ran into the brushy undergrowth to the south of Buck's driveway—towards Tom's house. *Too risky to shoot,* Buck thought.

The loud report woke both of the Strands, who sat up in bed and listened.

"The bear must have returned to Wiley's place," Tom said. "Hope Buck got it. Guess we'll find out what happened tomorrow morning," he added lying back down.

Clutching her robe about her with folded arms, Leah scolded Buck when he entered the door. "Buck, are you crazy going out there in the dark and shooting!? Our neighbors will probably call the police!"

"I don't think so; I told Tom Monday evening that we've had a bear visiting our place, and that I was going to shoot it if it came back."

"Did you hit it?"

"I think so; it fell out of a tree right after I shot."

"Where is it now!?"

"It ran into the bushes just south of our driveway—toward Strands' place. I'll let 'em know tomorrow morning. Right now, I'm going to try to get back to sleep...."

"I know it isn't going to be easy for you or Jamie to stay in on such a nice day, Leah, but don't go outside until I get home. After getting up this morning, I went out with the flashlight and saw some blood below the tree the bear fell out of. I didn't think following a blood trail into the bushes right before heading to work was a good idea, but, I did call the Strands to fill them in and tell them to not venture too far from the house today. I'm going to ask Russ Peters if he'll cover my sixth period class so I can leave early and head home to check things out. I should be home about 2:00. You know, it might be better if you and Jamie were away when I get home—maybe go visit the Andersons. I'll call you as soon as I find the bear or figure out where it headed. The good news is that, whether it's dead or wounded, it probably won't be coming back."

"Okay, but be careful, Buck. Why don't you ask Tom or another neighbor to search with you?"

"I will if I can find someone," he said heading for his truck.

Before Buck unlocked his classroom, he walked next door to Russ's room. "Hey, Russ...remember that bear I was telling you about on Monday?"

"Yeah."

"Well, it came back last night and went through our garbage again. When I went out with the shotgun, it ran up a tree. After I shot, it fell to the ground; but before I could get another shot off, it ran into some bushes by our driveway."

"Holy shit! So, you don't know if you killed it?"

"No...so I'm wondering if you'd be willing to cover my sixth period class so I could head home early and see if I can find it. I don't want a wounded bear nearby."

"Sure...but, Buck, you should have someone with you. Walking into the brush where there might be a wounded bear isn't the safest thing to do."

"Well, you know me, Russ—not the safest guy on the planet," Buck chuckled.

"I know! That's why I'm telling you to have someone with you."

Leah knew it was going to be difficult to keep Jamie inside on such a beautiful day, so after breakfast, she strapped Jamie into her safety seat and drove in to Missoula to run a few errands and grocery shop. While in the grocery store, Leah aisle shopped to take as much time as possible. It was worth it to her to put up with Jamie's asking if she could have what looked attractive to her from the cart.

Before heading for home, Leah pulled into McDonalds to treat Jamie to chicken nuggets and a small dish of soft vanilla ice cream. When they finished lunch, Leah got a coffee refill and watched Jamie climb around the interior playground. The longer she could extend the afternoon, the better.

After returning home and tucking Jamie in for her nap, she put the groceries away then called her friend, Sharon Anderson, and told her what was going on. She asked if she and Jamie could come over after Jamie's nap, until Buck called.

"Of course!" Sharon replied. "Lauren will be thrilled to see Jamie, and we can visit while the girls play. You may need a glass of wine!"

"Thanks again for watching my class, Russ," Buck said when Russ walked over to Buck's class at the beginning of sixth period. "I've taken roll, and they all have projects they're working on—*so you shouldn't have any problems*," Buck said in a voice loud enough for his students to hear. *"Right class!?"*

Heads nodded as students dug out their materials and assembled them on their desks.

"No problem, Buck. Just promise me you won't go looking for that bear by yourself," Russ said looking into Buck's eyes.

"I'll call my neighbor when I get home."

"Good," Russ nodded.

When Buck arrived home, he was relieved to see Leah's car gone. Entering the door, he spotted her note on the kitchen table: *"At Andersons; call me as soon as the coast is clear."* Buck picked up the phone and called the Strands' number: one...two...three rings...no answer. *Damn!* He thought about waiting for awhile and trying again but he didn't want Leah and Jamie to come home while he was looking for the bear, so he went upstairs, changed into his yard clothes and low cut boots, and loaded another slug into the shotgun before heading outside.

He located the patch of dried blood where the bear had fallen onto the ground, then began to follow the now dark specs of blood into the snowberry bushes south of the driveway. Carrying the gun chest high in case he had to shoot quickly, he slowly and cautiously followed the dark droplets, some of which were on the bushes; others on the ground. The retreating bear had made a pretty obvious swath as it ran through the brush. After each step, Buck stopped to listen for any sound; to look for any movement—his shotgun raised and ready. When he was about thirty yards into the bushes, he couldn't find any more droplets of blood, and couldn't see any more broken branches. It was as if the bear had suddenly disappeared. He slowly panned the area; then took one step backward, then another.

Suddenly, the bear emerged out of a hollow tree trunk, hidden by the snowberry bushes. It grabbed Buck's right leg with its paws and began chomping on his lower leg. It growled ferociously and Buck's leg was quickly covered in blood. He did his best to pull his leg from the bear's grasp, but couldn't. The bear's grasp was too strong. He feared he was too close to the bear to shoot without hitting his own leg, so he raised the butt of the rifle and smashed it against the bear's head. Seemingly unfazed, it continued to clutch his leg. Buck shoved the butt between his leg and the bear's mouth, pushing and prying with all his might. When the bear's claws briefly lost their grip on Buck's leg, he stepped back, lowered the barrel and fired two quick shots into the bear's head. **BOOM! BOOM!** The growling stopped; it lay still. As Buck stood there staring at the bear and shaking, he became aware of the bear's stench. It made him gag. He wrinkled his nose, turned away, and headed back through the brush toward the house. He couldn't believe what had just happened to him.

When he reached the porch, he set the gun down, and fearing the worst, slowly began to raise his bloody right pant leg. Strangely, he didn't feel any pain. He eased the pant leg up clearing his ankle, then his calf but saw no blood on his skin. There were some scratches and some redness, but no puncture wounds! *What the....! I gotta go check out the bear more closely.* But, before doing so, he went back inside, loaded two more slugs into the shotgun, then walked back through the brush to the bear. He placed the muzzle on the bear's open eye closest to him. Not a twitch. Assured the bear was dead, he grabbed the head of the bear and lifted it up. To his amazement, most of its lower jaw was missing! The few lower teeth that hadn't been shot away, hung unnaturally to what remained of the jaw. Both dried, dark blood and fresh, red blood were visible on the bear's mouth. *Holy shit...I must have shot its lower jaw off last night when it was in the tree! THANK GOD!!*

Returning to the house, and still shaking, Buck removed his boots and pants. He wiped the blood off his right boot with his pants, then washed the blood off the pants in the laundry room sink before tossing them and his work shirt into the washer. He started the washer, then went upstairs and turned on the shower. While the water ran over his still shaking body, he reflected back on what had just happened. *I was sooo lucky...thank you, Lord! What would have happened had I not shot its lower jaw off? What if I hadn't been able to get a shot off when it had my leg?*

Toweling off, he put his teaching clothes on again and called the Andersons.

"Hi, Sharon; this is Buck."

"*Buck!* Leah told me about the bea...*visitor*. Are you okay?"

"Yes, I'm fine."

"Leah will be so relieved...here she is."

"Buck...so glad you're okay. Did you find the bear?" she asked in a whisper so Jamie wouldn't hear.

"Well...kinda...it actually found *me*." He went on to describe what had happened.

"You are a lucky man, Buck Wiley." Then she added in a scolding voice, "You said you were going to find someone to go with you!"

"Well, I tried calling Tom, but no one was home. I'll talk to him when he gets home from work and have him help me load the bear into my truck when no kids are around. Won't take long for it to start smellin' up the place."

"I won't argue with that. We'll be home shortly; I'm so relieved you're okay, and that our scavenger won't be coming back. Love you! Bye."

After hanging up, Buck was heading to the laundry room to toss his clothes into the dryer when he heard the knock. It was Tom Strand still dressed in his business clothes. "Are you okay, Buck? My wife said she heard a couple shots right after she returned from the store this afternoon."

"Yes, I'm okay, but let me show you something." Buck stepped onto the porch and closed the door behind him. "You're not going to believe this...."

Dinner Date

"How'd it go?" Buck Wiley asked when Brady Romans, his roommate and assistant football coach entered their upstairs apartment about 6:30 pm on Monday, in mid-September, 1973.

"The scouting trip or the drive?" Brady responded.

"Ahh, the scouting report," Buck replied looking at Brady a bit puzzled.

"I think I got some good stuff, but let me tell you about the drive first. When I was just a few miles this side of Pomeroy, a big doe jumped off one of those banks above Highway 12, right in front of me. I didn't even have time to react. I hit her broadside and she rolled off the side of the highway down into the ditch. The bad news is that "Puke" has a new dent in her grill and hood; the good news is that we have some venison for our freezer."

"You mean, you...."

"Yeah, let's go out to your car and I'll show you."

Buck headed for the front of his 1965 blue Chevy Impala, parked in back of their apartment, to check out the damage. "As long as it still runs, it's okay by me. Isn't the first dent and probably won't be the last," Buck said with a shrug, walking back to the trunk.

Brady opened the trunk to reveal the large doe laying on her right side. "There was nobody behind me and I couldn't see another car coming either way, so I pulled your car off the side of the road nearby, walked back and gutted her out with my trusty Swiss Army knife."

"No one saw you?"

"I don't think so. A couple of cars passed above me on the road, but no one slowed down or stopped. When I was done gutting her, I backed your car to her, dragged her up onto the shoulder and lifted one end into the trunk; then the other. Man, I couldn't believe how heavy she was—even gutted out! I stopped along the river first chance I got, and washed off the gore. It's pretty warm out, but I knew I was just a few miles outside of town. If we get right to removing the hide, boning out the meat and getting it into the refrigerator, I think the meat will be fine."

"Okay, but we're going to have to do it upstairs in the kitchen," Buck said. "It's not hunting season yet, so if someone sees us working on her out here, we're toast."

Brady nodded. "I'll grab a blue tarp from the garage, run upstairs, and cover the kitchen floor."

Before lifting the doe out of the trunk, they looked around to see if any neighbors were about. Seeing none, Buck said, "If you grab the front legs, I'll grab the back legs and we'll lift on the count of three, okay? Ready...one...two... *threee*...." They both strained as they lifted the doe from the trunk to the ground. They both looked about again, then, waddling back and forth, schlepped the stiffening doe along the north side of their apartment house, then up the steps to their front door.

Brady set his end down just long enough to open the door, then, picking up the front legs again, began to lug the front quarters up the steep, narrow staircase. He tried to keep the doe's hooves from marking up the walls as he pulled the deer upward. Buck lifted and pushed the hind quarters up the stairs as Brady pulled. In short order, both were puffing, grunting and laughing at the absurd scenario.

Suddenly, Tony, the renter in the downstair's apartment came out of his adjacent front door to investigate the noisy commotion. *"Holy Shit!"* he exclaimed. The bewildered, baffled look on Tony's face made Brady laughed out loud.

Buck turned around when he heard Tony's gasp. "Hi, Tony. This doe jumped in front of Brady when he was driving back from Pomeroy—we're just getting it upstairs so we can skin it and bone out the meat. You can help us if you want," Buck added in an attempt to put him at ease.

"Ahh...no...that's okay," he replied as if attempting determine if this was actually occurring.

"No problem...hey, would you mind closing our front door?" Buck asked.

"Ah...sure...okay," Tony replied before hastily retreating to his apartment and closing his door.

Tony's astonished stares and hasty retreat made Brady and Buck roar with laughter, as they continued their struggle to pull and push the buck up the stairs and onto the tarp in the kitchen. Once over the tarp, they set the carcass down, then stood up straight and stretched out their backs, while catching their breath.

"You know what, before we slice and dice, we should take some pictures of it with your camera," Brady suggested after spotting Buck's camera on the kitchen counter. "How about one on the couch with your arm around it? We can put a towel under it."

Buck laughed and headed down the hallway to grab a dirty towel from the bathroom. He returned and folding the towel in half, laid it on the nearest end of the old, worn avocado green couch. "Okay, let's try to sit her up." They hefted the carcass up onto the couch, then Buck sat down beside it and put his right arm around the deer.

"Perfect!" Brady grinned pushing the button on top of Buck's Kodak Instamatic. "Man, I'd love to see the look on the face of the person who develops this picture!" Brady laughed.

"Me, too," Buck replied. "Okay, let's get this critter back onto the kitchen floor and take care of business. I'll grab some of my hunting gear from my closet." He returned with his hunting knife and a folded up saw. "If you hold its head steady, I'll cut through the fur around its neck with my hunting knife, so we can cut the head off with the bone saw."

Brady was surprised by how tough the doe's hide was. It took a lot of effort for Buck to cut all around the neck.

"Okay, if you hand me that bone saw, I'll severe the head," Buck said. The small handsaw cut through the spine much quicker than the knife had through the fur. "There we go," sighed Buck detaching the head with one final thrust of the saw. "Would you mind taking this down and putting it in my trunk? Wrap the towel we just used around it so no one sees it. I'll start skinning it while you're doing that."

When Brady returned, he pulled the doe's hide away from one side of the carcass while Buck separated it from the meat with his hunting knife using short downward strokes. After cutting the hide away from the front and rear legs, he began to cut away large chunks of meat from the bones. "Here," he said handing a large chunk from a rear quarter to Brady. "Just put these in serving bowls for now so we can get it in the refrigerator. We'll clean it up later after the meat has chilled."

After all the meat was removed from one side, they rolled the carcass over onto the hide to complete the opposite side.

"Thanks," Buck said standing up straight and stretching his back again. "Man, glad that's done!" He placed his knife in the kitchen sink and asked Brady to help him fold the hide over the carcass, then roll up the remains in the tarp and carry the works to his trunk. "A bit lighter now, huh!" Buck said holding his end of the tarp up off the stairs and walking backwards. "Tomorrow, I'll talk to one of the players, whose dad is a butcher here in town. After we clean up the meat, we can ask him to grind it into hamburger for us."

After tossing the rolled up tarp into the trunk, Buck closed it. "Since you've been driving all day, I'll go get rid of this as soon as it gets dark. Right now, let's clean up, then we'll walk over to *Der Litten Haus* for some dinner. On me tonight. You can fill me in on what you learned about Cashmere."

After they placed their dinner orders, Buck asked Brady how his scouting venture went.

"Well, I wore my jogging stuff to Cashmere, so I'd look like I was just jogging around the football practice area. I'd stop to rest and stretch when I got to different coaching stations. One key item I picked up on from their offensive linemen was the calls for their blocking schemes. Their guards yell, *"yellow"* when they're going to double team; blue when they're going to cross-block."

"Nice!" Buck exclaimed. "That will be a huge help to our defensive linemen and linebackers! How do they compare size-wise to us?"

"Their linemen are about the same size as our guys, and their backs are just average sized. Their QB is an okay passer. I watched him throw several passes—mostly look-ins and post routes to his split end. He threw most of the passes I saw to the same wide receiver, who set up on both ends of the line. Their QB isn't nearly as quick and shifty as McQuarter is for us. They line up in the "I" formation, and seem to run the ball most of the time.

"I didn't get to see their defensive sets, but I think we should be able to move the ball on them with our speed, and the pressure McQuarter will put on their corners and halfbacks when he rolls out to pass or run."

"Nicely done, Brady! I sure appreciate you driving all the way over there, not gettin' caught, and driving all the way back in the same day. *And*, I might add, bringing home some venison to boot!"

"No problem," Brady smiled. "Hey, after we get the venison ground up, we should give Patsy and Bethany a call, and invite them over for burgers. We haven't seen them since the new teacher orientation."

"Great idea! It has been pretty much all work and no play the past few weeks. Of course, unbeknownst to them, they'll have to help us *package* the burger before we can cook them one."

"Oh, my God—that's hilarious!" Brady chuckled. "And, we won't be lying to them—we'll be inviting them over for burgers," Brady added as their dinners arrived.

After dinner, they returned to the apartment and started cleaning up the venison. Brady washed off the pieces of meat under the kitchen faucet and placed them in a dish rack to dry off. Buck, using his hunting knife, trimmed off any fat and gristle, then placed the cleaned meat into one of his hunting meat sacks.

Mr. Draper greeted Buck and Brady from behind his meat counter, as they entered his butcher shop the following afternoon after football practice. "My son told me you have some venison you'd like ground into burger?"

"Yes, please," Buck answered. "Seems Brady here is into 'road kill'."

"Hey, she jumped off a bank, right in front of me!" Brady quickly added shrugging his shoulders with his hands widespread.

Mr. Draper chuckled. "How much fat you want in the burger?"

"Let's go 10 per cent," Buck said.

"Would you like the burger wrapped?"

Buck looked at Brady and grinned. "No, we can do that."

"Okay," Mr. Draper said filling out an order slip. He glanced at the large calendar on his counter. "Let's see…I could have that done by… Saturday afternoon."

"Great!" Buck replied glancing back at Brady with a smile. "Oh, we may need a freezer locker after we wrap the burger; how much would that be?"

"A small locker would be five bucks a month."

"Sounds good," Buck replied. "Put us down for one."

"Okay, let's weigh your meat and I'll give you an approximate cost on the burger."

Buck handed the blood-stained sack of venison to the butcher then glanced over at Brady. "The small freezer in our refrigerator won't be big enough for all this burger—until we get it down a ways.

Mind going in with me on the locker?"

"Not at all," Brady responded.

"Good luck against Cashmere on Friday," Mr. Draper said as the coaches headed for the door. "My wife and I will be there cheering from the stands."

"Thanks, Mr. Draper."

"We sure enjoy coaching your son! He's having a great season," Brady added before they left the shop.

As they walked to Buck's car, Brady said, "Hey, when we get back to the apartment, let's call Patsy and Bethany to invite them over for burgers on Saturday night. This will give them enough notice before they make other plans."

"Good idea," Buck replied.

"Hi, Patsy, this is Brady Romans...good, thanks. How are you.... Hey, I'm calling to see if you and Bethany would like to come over to join Buck and me for burgers Saturday evening." Brady waited while Patsy asked Bethany if she would be available. "Great! ...how about 5:30? ...okay, we'll see you Saturday at 5:30.... You too, teach up a storm this week. Bye.

"Great! They'll be here Saturday at 5:30. I can't wait to see their faces when they walk up the stairs and see the mound of burger on the table!"

"I'll pick up some plastic wrap, butcher paper and tape this week so we can wrap up a storm after they get here. We'll put some packages in the freezer and keep the rest in our fridge until we can take it to our meat locker," Buck said.

"Sounds good," Brady replied. "Well, think I'll finish correcting the last of the papers I brought home and prepare my classes for the rest of the week."

"Yeah, I need to do some 'a that as well."

"Hey, nice win last night you guys!" Mr. Draper shouted, as the coaches entered his shop Saturday afternoon. "Man, your defense really shut down their offense."

"Thanks," Buck replied with a grin. "We had a pretty good scouting report on them thanks to Brady here."

They discussed the game a bit, then Buck asked Mr. Draper how much they owed him for the venison burger.

"This one's on the house!" Mr. Draper replied. "You guys are renting a locker; that's good enough for now."

"Are you sure!?" Buck asked.

"Yep—just keep up the great coaching."

"Thank you so much, Mr. Draper!" the coaches chimed before exiting his shop.

About 5:00 pm, Buck said, "Let's move the kitchen table out into the middle of the kitchen so we can all work around it." He then covered the table top with plastic wrap before upending the five gallon bucket and dumping the mounded venison burger onto the table.

"Oh, my gosh, that's a lot of hamburger!" Brady gasped staring at the large mound of burger in the middle of the table. "The girls are going to freak out when they see it."

"I know. I'll take their picture when they get here—which should be in about...25 minutes. Just enough time to clean up a bit and get the place ready for them."

"Come on in!" shouted Brady from the kitchen when he heard the knock at the front door downstairs.

"We're here," announced Patsy.

"Welcome! Come on up," Brady grinned from the top of the stairs. "Buck and I are up here, slaving over dinner."

When the girls got to the top of the stairs and saw the mountain of burger on the table, they froze for a moment with their mouths open and looked at one another.

"Oh, my God!" Patsy gasped in awe.

"We wanted to make sure we had enough to fill you gals up," chuckled Buck. "Here, let me take your coats; then I'll take a few pics before we get started. Hi, Bethany, I'm glad you could join us this evening."

"Me too...I think. I've never had to wrap hamburger before eating it," she said looking at the mound and wrapping supplies beside it.

Buck laughed and took her coat. "Okay, girls, if you'll stand on that side of the table, I'll get a picture before we begin wrapping the burger."

"I want a print when you get them developed," Patsy said. "I want to show my friends and family what single women do for fun in Clarkston on a Saturday night."

They all enjoyed a good laugh.

Buck handed the girls dish towels that they could use as aprons. "Okay, I think the easiest way to do this is if we all have a certain job. How about if...Patsy, you tear off plastic pieces about this size," he demonstrated, "and just lay them down on the table. I'll make small mounds of burger that are about a pound each and wrap the plastic around them. Brady, you can package them in butcher paper like this," he demonstrated tearing off a piece of the butcher paper and wrapping the mound diagonally. "Bethany, you can secure the packages with tape."

"Okay, I'll stand next to Buck," Patsy said holding the plastic."

"And, I'll stand next to Patsy so Buck can pass the mounds to me; then I'll pass them to you, Bethany," added Brady.

"I'm ready," announced Bethany.

While they wrapped the venison burger, they talked about their students, staff and teaching experiences since meeting one another at the new teachers' luncheon at the Elks Club in late August. Bethany and Patsy, both first year teachers, related how much time it took them to prepare their lessons, and how exhausted they were by the end of each day. Buck and Brady, who had two years of teaching experience before coming to Clarkston, talked about their classes and how much time and energy it took to prepare the football team for upcoming opponents. The time flew by quickly as they all enjoyed this opportunity to break away from their demanding schedules and socialize with other single teachers their age.

"Last one," Buck announced handing Brady the last plastic-wrapped mound of burger. "After I wash my hands, I'll start to put the packages in the freezer and the fridge. If you gals like the venison burger, you can take some home if you'd like."

"Oh, thanks, Brady," Patsy replied removing the towel from her waist.

"I'll give you a quick tour of our roomy 'digs' here before I help Buck in the kitchen; then you gals relax while we cook up the burgers. This is obviously the living room," Brady gestured with his left hand before leading the girls down the short, narrow hallway. "Buck's room is on the left; mine's here on the right. The bathroom, in case you need to use it, is straight ahead. Well, there you have it—that didn't take long did it!?" Brady added a bit apologetically.

"Hey, I get it," Patsy said. "Before I moved into the rental house with Bethany, my apartment was *tiny*: one very small bedroom, a narrow, one-butt kitchen, and an equally small sitting space. But, it was all I could afford on my first year salary."

"Yeah, combining our monthly rent to move into that house was definitely the way to go," Bethany added. "The apartment I was renting was so small and depressing.

"Hey, Buck, need any help in there?" she asked as they walked past the kitchen and back into the living room.

"No, you gals just relax in there while Brady and I get things ready. We're here to wait on you gals!"

"*Riiiiigggghhhhtttt!*" the girls chuckled.

Brady headed into the kitchen to begin setting the table, while Buck placed the venison patties into the iron skillet. They sizzled as they contacted the hot oil and within seconds, the aroma of cooking meat permeated the apartment.

"You gals like salt and pepper?" Buck asked.

"Yes," they chimed.

Brady opened the window on the north side of the kitchen for ventilation, as the kitchen had no fan.

"Okay, dinner is served," announced Buck from the stove.

The girls entered the kitchen and took a seat at the table now covered by a table cloth, place settings with paper napkins and glasses of water. Each plate had a hamburger on it; a separate plate offered lettuce, tomato and onion. A bowl of salad was in the center of the table accompanied by bottles of French and Italian salad dressings and bottles of ketchup and mustard. A steaming bowl of green beans with a serving spoon in it sat on top of a trivet. Salt and pepper shakers completed the center display.

"Help yourself to lettuce, tomato, ketchup and mustard," Brady offered. A brief minute of silence ensued as they dressed their burgers and dished up salad and green beans.

Bethany picked up her hamburger and took her first bite, chewing slowly and deliberately, as if analyzing the taste before saying anything. "Hmmm, this is really good!" she said as if surprised. "I've never had venison burger before."

"Me, neither," Patsy added chewing her first bite. "I really like it!"

"Good!" Buck smiled. "We'll send you gals home with some. Just save room for dessert because we're taking you out for ice cream after dinner."

"Don't tell me we're going to have to milk the cow first!" Bethany said dryly which made them all laugh.

Now that both girls were comfortable with their first venison burger, the dinner conversations about teaching, their families, and favorite hobbies flowed easily. Their frequent giddy laughter made it obvious they were enjoying this unique dinner date.

"So, which one of you shot the deer?" asked Patsy.

All-Nighter

After I exited the warmth of the sleeping bag the third time, I could tell that it was beginning to get light. To the east, the sky was a deep red. I then looked north toward the clearing, slowly scanning it. That's when I noticed a dark object moving slowly about two or three hundred yards out. I focused on the object and as my eyes adjusted to the faint light, I could tell there were several dark objects moving slowly.

"Buck! I think I see some deer," I whispered excitedly. ...

Buck and I had driven over five hours from Clarkston to the Bearmouth, east of Missoula, after our football game with the Colville Indians. Buck Wiley, the head football coach, had asked me after our coaches meeting the previous week, if I wanted to go deer hunting with him. I explained to him that I'd only hunted once back in high school, and that I didn't have a hunting license, a rifle or any hunting gear.

"That's okay, Brady. You won't need a hunting license because you won't have a rifle—you'll just be tagging along with me. And I've got some extra hunting clothes I can lend you. Do you have a pair of boots?"

"Yeah, but just some cheap J.C. Penney leather work boots. They're not very warm, but would probably do."

"How about long underwear and gloves?"

"Yes, for snow skiing."

"Good...and you can wear your red ski jacket. I have an extra pair of wool pants and wool socks and an extra hunting shirt."

"Well, okay then," I replied excitedly. "Thanks for asking me!"

Neither of us felt sleepy as we were still jacked-up from the close game. The Colville Indians out-sized our team, the Bantams, but got off to a sluggish start due in part to their nearly four hour ride to Clarkston on a school bus. Our team was able to score three touchdowns before halftime; then outlast the Indians for the 21-14 victory in the rainy, cold conditions.

As Buck drove east over rainy US 12, we debriefed the game, talked about injured players, teammates who could take their places next week if need be, and discussed game plans for our next opponent, the Pullman Grayhounds.

Halfway up the summit to Lolo Pass, the rain turned to snow, and required more of Buck's concentration. It snowed lightly but steadily the rest of the way to Missoula.

It was 4:20 am when Buck topped off the gas tank in East Missoula; 5:10 when we took the Bearmouth exit from I-90. I estimated there were about five inches of snow on the ground when I stepped out of Buck's blue 1968 Chevy Impala to open the gate to Don Baker's ranch where Buck boarded his mare, Misty.

"Just leave the gate open, Brady; we'll be heading back out shortly," Buck directed as he drove the car through the entrance and parked beside a small metal shed nearby.

The chilly night air was a shock after traveling so long in the toasty car. It seemed to go right through my layered clothing. *"Brrrr!"* I exclaimed with arms crossed on my chest as I approached the car. I grabbed my red ski jacket, red and white stocking hat and black leather ski gloves from the back seat where they'd been covering Buck's rifle, and quickly put them on. Buck had already zipped up his heavy hunting coat.

He singled out a small key on his key chain and handed it to me. "If you unlock the padlock to this tack shed, I'll go give Misty some oats; then lead her out."

As I waited for Buck and Misty, I panned the surroundings of the ranch. I couldn't believe how stark everything looked now compared to July, when I'd first driven there with Buck. All the deciduous leaves had fallen and the white snow made everything look so bleak and frigid. I became conscious of my toes which were already tingling from the cold. *If they're already feeling this cold, how am I going to hunt in this snow?*

As Buck led Misty toward the tack shed, I was surprised at how thick and shaggy her coat was now. Her short, sleek coat had looked so shiny back in July.

"If you hold her lead rope, I'll brush her down before saddling her," Buck said. Misty turned her nose toward my coat sniffing to see if she recognized my scent.

"Do you remember me, Misty? Probably not with all the layers I'm wearing," I said while stroking her face and neck. "A little colder now than last summer, huh!" I was still a little intimidated by Misty's size and the memory of her trying to knock me off her bare back by walking over close to a tree.

Buck returned the grooming brush to the shed and placed a thick saddle blanket on her back, followed by a heavy leather saddle with bags on each side. I watched as he positioned the saddle, tightened the cinch, and fastened the chest strap and crupper. He placed some baling twine and a small folded-up saw in the right saddle bag and tied a curled rope to the right side of the saddle.

"Brady, can you get the sleeping bag out of the trunk and tie it to the back of the saddle? Given how cold it is, it may come in handy later."

"Sure."

Buck grabbed a box of ammunition from the back seat and put it in the left saddle bag; then grabbed his .270 from the back seat, and slid it into the scabbard secured to the left side of the saddle. Ducking into the shed again, he grabbed Misty's bridle. "Head down!" he commanded before giving Misty the cold bit, sliding her bridle up her face and over her ears, then buckling the throat latch. "Good girl!" praised Buck patting her neck.

"Okay, here's what we're gonna do, Brady. I'm going to ride Misty back out the gate and down the road that goes under the freeway. I'll cross the bridge over the river, then take a left down a siding road. Follow me in the car—just not too closely or you might spook Misty. I'll show you where to park the car when we get there. Oh, and could you please close the gate after you drive though?"

"Okay," I replied.

I enjoyed the warmth from the car's heater while following Buck. He was hunkered down in the saddle attempting to shield his face and body from the bitter cold. I watched him turn left on the siding road, and when I saw him point to the right side of the road, I pulled the car over, turned off the lights and the ignition, and stepped out into the frigid air.

"Go ahead and lock it, Brady—just *don't lose the keys*! That would not be good!"

"Keys are in the right pocket of my ski jacket, Buck, and I'm zipping the pocket closed."

"There's a game trail over this way that I'll try to follow; just walk in the horse's tracks as we head up—walking will help you keep warm."

I hoped this would be the case as my toes were already feeling numb. *These uninsulated leather boots just aren't adequate for this cold weather. I'm so glad I brought my lined ski gloves; at least my hands should be warm!*

As my eyes adjusted, I was amazed at how well I could actually see because of the snow and the faint moonlight. I had no trouble keeping track of Misty and Buck. After about 100 yards, the climb grew steeper. *Buck was right, I am getting warmer—even my toes.*

"Brady!" Buck called in a loud whisper. "Keep headin' up the slope...I'm going to ride over toward the trees on our right and see if I can catch some fresh deer tracks."

I could kind of tell where the game trail was because the snow looked slightly recessed in those spots. But, it got confusing at times because there appeared to be other game trails in places that intersected the one I was on, before branching off in slightly different directions. Every now and then, some fallen debris would block the trail I was following, and I'd have to relocate it after finding a way around the obstacle.

About a third of the way up the slope, I was startled by a thunderous explosion behind me. It made the hair on the back of my neck stand up and my heart race.

"Just a coyote!" announced Buck ejecting the spent shell. "We'll pick him up on the way out. I can sell his hide."

"Man, that scared the shit out of me, Buck!" I exclaimed, attempting to slow my rapid heart rate."

"Sorry, Brady."

I walked back to where Buck and Misty were standing and stared down at the motionless coyote.... "I didn't know coyotes' fur got so fluffy and white during the winter!"

"Yeah, it's really soft too. Take your hand out of your glove and feel it."

"Oh, my gosh, it's *really* soft!"

Buck loaded another shell into the chamber, engaged the safety, and slid his rifle back into the scabbard. Rather than remount, he led Misty by her lead rope. "Think I'll walk the rest of the way to the top as well," he said. "It's steep and too slippery for Misty with me on her back. Besides, the walking will help warm me up. Man, it's cold!"

After another 45 minutes of climbing and stopping periodically to rest, we reached the top of the steep hill. About seventy-five yards directly ahead of us was a stand of trees, and to the north of there, what appeared to be a large clearing.

"This is perfect!" exclaimed Buck tying Misty to a nearby tree. "If any deer wander out into that clearing, they won't be able to see us." He untied the sleeping bag from the back of the saddle and unrolled it on the snow. "We'll take turns warming up in the sleeping bag so we don't get too cold while we wait for daylight."

... Buck wriggled out of the sleeping bag, grabbed his rifle from the scabbard and looked through the scope at where I was pointing. "Good eye, Brady! There's one pretty good-sized buck and four or five does." Buck handed me his rifle. "Here, take a look. A little bit more to your right...do you see 'em?"

"Oh, yeah, now I see 'em. That buck does look good-sized."

"Well, I'm goin' for the big fella," Buck exclaimed dragging the sleeping bag over to a log and lying on his belly. He rested the rifle's stock on a downed tree trunk and looked through his scope. "It's about a three hundred yard shot...come on...turn sideways...there...." The roar of Buck's rifle made me jump even though I was expecting the shot. The loud report echoed off the surroundings. "Damn! Missed him," hissed Buck loading another shell into the chamber. He steadied the rifle and fired again. **BOOM**! "Darn it! At least they're stayin' put...they can't figure out what's goin' on. Brady, get more ammo out of the left saddle bag will ya!"

I hustled over to Misty, removed my gloves to undo the straps of the saddle bag, and rushed the ammo box back to Buck, who quickly reloaded the magazine.

"Okay, if I don't hit him this next shot, you take a couple of shots."

All of a sudden, I felt nervous. I hadn't shot a hunting rifle since my senior year in high school. The nervousness combined with my chilled hands made me shake. *Shit, there's no way I'll be able to hold the rifle steady!*

Buck concentrated and fired another round. **BOOM!** "Shit!" Buck stood up and handed me his rifle. "Okay, you take a couple of shots,

Brady. Safety's on...when you're ready to shoot, just slide it forward and squeeze the trigger."

I lay down on the sleeping bag, rested the rifle stock on the log and located the buck in the scope. I placed the cross hairs on the buck's side, took a deep breath, exhaled, then breathed in and held it in an attempt to stop shaking. Trying not to anticipate the loud roar I knew was coming, I pulled the trigger. **BOOM!**

"He's still standing, Brady! Take another shot."

I concentrated and tried my best to steady the rifle before pulling the trigger again. **BOOM!**

"He's still there, take another shot."

"Here, Buck," I said handing the rifle back to Buck. "I can't even hold the rifle steady. I'm shaking too much."

Buck inserted two more shells into the magazine. Lying back down, he squeezed off another round that missed the deer, quickly ejected the spent shell casing, and loaded another shell into the chamber. The rifle roared again. **BOOM!** "Got him!"

I looked out into the clearing and saw the buck roll over onto its back. He was moving his legs as if attempting to right himself; then he rolled onto his right side and was still.

"Good shot, Buck!"

"Thanks!" Buck replied standing up and heading over to Misty. *"Finally!"* He slid his rifle into the scabbard, untied the lead rope and mounted Misty. "I'm going to ride out and drag it back here...be back in a few."

I watched Buck ride out into the clearing and could see the bewildered does looking back to where the buck had been standing. They bounced off a ways as Buck neared them, then stopped and looked back as if waiting for the buck to rejoin them. Soon Buck was riding back dragging the buck in the snow behind Misty.

"Oh, my gosh, that *is* a big buck!" I exclaimed.

"Yeah...pretty good-sized four point Mulie," Buck replied smiling. "And now the fun part begins," he added as he removed the folded-up saw from the right saddle bag. He took off his coat, laid it on top of the sleeping bag and rolled up his shirt sleeves. Rolling the deer onto its back, he removed a knife from his pocket and unfolded it. "Take hold of its front legs and keep its belly facing up," Buck directed. "I'll do a quick gut job and we can get outta here."

I watched Buck start at the buck's rear and cut upward. As he did so, the buck's innards began to bulge outward through the seam, steaming as they met the frigid air. When he'd cut up to the breastplate, he attempted to cut through it with his knife, but unable to do so, used the bone saw. He then extended the seam to the buck's throat.

"Now the windpipe," Buck said breathing hard. Reaching upward, he severed the windpipe then, placing his knife on the snow to the right side of the deer, used both hands to pull the steaming innards downward. Occasionally, he'd grab his knife and cut along the insides of the rib cage to release the stubborn innards. Mixed in with Buck's grunts and groans as he labored, were the wet sounds from the blood in the deer's cavity as he cut and pulled the innards toward him. "Oh, it's a bloody business, Brady!"

After he'd pulled the guts downward from the deer's chest cavity, he moved the pile outside the carcass and to the side. He made a couple quick cuts near the buck's hind section and the gut pile was free. Steam rose from the pile and the deer's open cavity.

"There...we'll skin and bone it later," Buck said standing up straight to stretch out his back, still breathing hard.

"Oh my God, look at the size of that bullet hole!" I said in amazement now that the buck was on its side.

"Yeah, the exit hole is always larger," Buck said. He rubbed his knife blade on the edge of a stump and then in the snow to remove as much of the blood, tissue and hair as he could before releasing the blade and putting the knife back into his pocket. He knelt down and, grabbing handfuls of snow, wiped off his bloody arms, then rubbed his hands together. "Brrrr!" he exclaimed moving his shirt sleeves down and buttoning them.

When he turned back toward the clearing to get his jacket from the sleeping bag, he exclaimed, "Brady! Look! The does are headin' this way." Buck hustled over to Misty, pulled out his rifle, slid the bolt back to make sure there was a live round in the chamber and handed it to me. "Okay, safety's on..plug one of 'em!"

I watched in amazement as the still confused does continued toward us in single file at a fast walk. About fifteen yards away, the does must have caught our alien scents because they veered to their left.

"Shoot!" urged Buck.

I raised the rifle and fired as the second doe passed in front of me. I hadn't had time to fix the crosshairs behind the deer's front shoulder—I just fired when I saw brown in the scope. The doe lurched forward, ran about ten yards and fell. I stood there for a second. *My first deer!* I headed toward the doe and was shocked by the extent of the blood trail. The snow was bright red leading up to the doe, where a patch of red snow was widening underneath her. Her dark eyes were open but appeared vacant—focused on nothing.

Buck walked over. "Heart shot," he said. "Nice shot!"

"Thanks, Buck," I replied grinning but still stunned by what I'd just done.

"Now, it's *your* turn to get your hands dirty," Buck declared putting his rifle back into the scabbard. "Here's my knife."

I removed my jacket and placed it on the sleeping bag as Buck had done, rolled up my sleeves and positioned the doe onto its back. "You'll have to tell me what to do, Buck; I've never done this before."

"Here, let me get you started," he offered, making an incision down by the doe's anus. "Now, put your two fingers underneath the hide...like this...palm facing up and lift upward like this. Keep the blade flat as you cut upward. You do *not* want to puncture the guts."

"Sorry this is taking me so long," I apologized slowly working my way to the breastplate.

"That's okay; it gets easier and faster with experience. Cut up as far as you can with your knife," Buck encouraged. "Now, put the knife aside and use the saw to cut through the breastplate. Good. Okay, reach way up and find the windpipe. Grab it with your left hand and cut through it with the knife."

As I reached up into the deer's cavity to find the doe's windpipe, the warm innards felt good on my hands. "Now I know why you like to do this," I chuckled. When I found the windpipe, I cut through it, put the knife beside the doe and began to pull the innards toward me with both hands. Everything felt smooth and slippery. It became obvious quickly that I had to use the knife blade to release the innards from the cavity. "Man, this isn't easy," I said grunting as I ran the blade along the inside of the rib cage while pulling with my left hand.

"Push the guts away from one side with your left hand while you cut; then switch hands and do the same on the other side," coached Buck. "This will help give you a bit more room to work.... Maybe I'll climb back in the sleeping bag; looks like it might take you awhile," Buck kidded leaning against a nearby tree.

"Don't abandon me now; I may need your help," I gasped pulling as hard as I could, hoping everything would just come loose. I couldn't believe how much work this was. I was breathing hard and actually beginning to sweat. My hands were warm as long as I kept them inside the carcass, but as soon as I pulled them out, they instantly got very cold. Finally, after much effort and *a lot* more time than it took Buck, I was able to release the gut bag and move it to the side of the doe.

"Good job, Brady! Here, I'll show you how to cut around all that stuff down there so you don't get urine and feces on the meat." Buck took the knife. "If you were going to skin and bone out you deer here, you'd want to pull the carcass away from the gut pile a ways to protect the meat. But we're going to leave the hides on these critters so we can drag them to the hill and roll them down. We'll skin them when we get back to Clarkston. They'll stay plenty cold in the trunk."

I cleaned off the saw blade as best I could, then using snow, washed off as much blood as I could from my arms and hands. I rolled down my sleeves, buttoned the cuffs, put on my red ski jacket and then my gloves. "Man, does it ever feel good to put on my jacket and gloves again! Thanks for helping me get through all that, Buck."

"My pleasure, Brady," Buck smiled.

Buck tied the rope around the necks of both deer, mounted Misty, wrapped the other end of the rope around the saddle horn and began to drag both deer toward the hillside. "Just walk behind them," Buck directed. "Let me know if they get snagged on anything."

When Buck had dragged the deer to the brink of the hillside, he dismounted and removed the rope from the saddle horn. "Okay, let's untie 'em and begin rolling 'em down the slope. When they get caught on something, we'll drag them clear and start them rollin' again."

"Is this how you *tenderize* deer meat?" I chuckled.

"Got that right," Buck laughed. "At least we have snow, which makes it a lot easier to drag them."

When Buck was near where he'd shot the coyote, he mounted Misty and rode over to it. "I'm going to remove the pelt here," explained Buck. "Just hold Misty's lead rope and catch your breath for awhile."

After Buck finished removing the hide, he secured the pelt to the left side of the saddle with the attached leather straps, then we continued rolling the deer down the hill until the slope began to flatten out. I could see the tracks we'd made on our way up earlier that morning.

"Let's tie the deer together again so Misty can drag them to the car; then we're going to have to cut off the buck's antlers so we can fit both animals into the trunk."

When we reached the car, Buck dismounted, untied the rope, wound it up and, using the leather straps attached to the saddle, tied it to the right side of the saddle. He then pulled the saw out of the right saddle bag. "This isn't the easiest job; so we'll trade off." He sawed a groove through the hide at about a thirty degree angle in front of the skull below the antlers, and another behind the skull toward the antlers. "Okay, try to maintain this same angle as you saw," he instructed.

I sawed until my right arm was tired and I was breathing hard; then Buck took a turn. It was a lot more work than I thought it would be. After three turns each, Buck grabbed the antlers and attempted to break them free from the skull. "Not quite enough," he said. "One more turn each and we should be home free."

After the next rotation, Buck grabbed the front antlers again and pressed downward on them with his weight. They fell forward with a loud snap. "Just cut the skin a bit more right there and they should come free," Buck coached. "Good job!" he added standing up tall and stretching out his back. He sawed a ways into a nearby branch to remove some of the bone debris from the saw blade, then used snow to wipe it clean before folding it up and placing it back into the right saddle bag. "Okay, if you'll get those car keys and open the trunk, we'll see if we're strong enough to lift this big fella into the trunk. The doe shouldn't be a problem. If you grab his front legs, I'll grab the back legs. Ready...one, two, three, *lift!*"

"Man, even without his innards, he's really heavy!" I exclaimed.

We had no trouble hefting the much lighter doe into the trunk but as Buck had suspected, we weren't able to fit in the antlers. "If this wasn't such a nice rack, I'd just leave it here," Buck said eyeing them. He thought a moment. "I'll just put them on the floor in the back seat."

Buck looked around to make sure we'd picked up everything. "Okay, just follow me back to the ranch the same way we came over. I'll get a head start while you warm up the car and defrost the windshield."

"It'll be my pleasure to get the car heated up!" I replied from the driver's seat, kicking the chassis to remove some of the snow from my feet.

When I pulled into the ranch, Buck was removing the tack from Misty and returning items to their places in the tack shed. "Just leave the car running so it continues to heat up. Let's put Misty back in the corral; I'll give her some oats, and then we can head for Clarkston."

Buck poured some oats into a large dish near the corral and placed it in front of Misty, who immediately scooped in a mouthful of oats with her lips and began to munch. "Good job, girl!" Buck complimented patting her on the neck. "Behave yourself 'til I get back in a couple weeks. We'll leave this corral gate open so she can head out to the pasture when she's done.

"If you wouldn't mind drivin' first, Brady, I'll get some shut-eye, then I'll drive the rest of the way to Clarkston."

"Sounds good," I said removing my hat, coat and gloves before sliding back into the driver's seat. Buck took off his gloves and coat, got in the back seat, and bunching his coat for a pillow, lay down.

I relished the warmth as the car's heater drove out the remaining chill, but it didn't take long before I began to feel sleepy. We'd been up nearly 30 hours after a full week of teaching, coaching and guiding our team to a victory over Colville. Buck was sawing logs within five minutes of lying down, and by the time we reached the Van Buren exit about 40 miles west of Bearmouth, I was fighting to stay awake.

I've got to get some coffee before heading for Lolo Pass, I thought to myself.

I finally found a restaurant on Brooks Street and walked inside.

"A large coffee please—with some milk in it," I asked the hostess.

"Will that be for here or to go?"

"To go, please."

Ahhh, that tastes so good! I thought relishing a sip of the hot coffee before heading back out into the cold. I opened the driver's door, set the steaming styrofoam cup on the car's roof while I removed my coat; then climbed in placing the cup on the dash.

Stirring from the backseat, Buck asked, "Everything okay?"

"Yep; just got some coffee," I replied fastening my seatbelt. "Go back to sleep; I'll wake you after we cross the summit." I took another sip of coffee then turned right on Brooks heading for Lolo Pass.

Fortunately, the highway department had recently plowed and sanded Hwy 12. It was still slow going with all its curves, but once the coffee kicked in, I kind of got my second wind. I was still a bit hyped-up from my first hunt with Buck and feeling good inside that I'd not only survived the frigid elements but had shot and field dressed my first deer.

As we approached Lowell, Idaho, however, I began to fade and get sleepy again. I pulled off the highway at the first restaurant I saw just west of Lowell and woke Buck.

After washing up in the restroom, we wolfed down our tasty hamburgers and fries, then, with full tummies, returned to the car. I eagerly got in the backseat to let Buck finish the drive to Clarkston. I rolled up my jacket for a pillow and when I closed my eyes, this morning's images began to stream through my mind: *walking up the snowy slope in the dark, Buck shooting the coyote, seeing the deer in the faint morning light, the roar of the rifle when we shot, its echo off the surroundings, running back to Misty to get more ammo, the buck rolling onto its back and kicking its legs as if trying to get up, Misty dragging it back in the snow, gutting it out; the does trotting toward us, shooting my first deer, the feeling of its innards as I field dressed it, rolling the deer down the hill to the car, lifting them into the trunk....*

The Bear Den

"**A**ny questions regarding this important mission...your objec-tives...your roles...?" asked the CO. "Okay, be back here at 0300 hours prepared to head out; we'll give you any recon updates at that time. Dismissed!"

Private First class John Wiley and fellow Army Ranger, Nick Neilson exited the briefing regarding tomorrow morning's pre-dawn mission to attack a Taliban force south of Kabul, Afghanistan.

"I'm feeling a bit nervous about this mission," Nick said as they walked back toward their barracks. "It seems more complex than others we've been on."

"Yeah, I always feel a bit nervous and even some fear before a mission like this one. It helps me to recall the time my dad convinced me to crawl into a bear's den to see if the bear he'd shot was dead."

"What!? Your dad talked you into going into a bear's den, where there was a wounded bear?"

"Yeah, it happened the morning of my first elk hunt with my dad, when I was twelve....

"Mornin' Son," my dad greeted when I shuffled into our ranch house kitchen at 5:15 am, wearing my camo pants and long john top.

"Mornin', Dad," I replied yawning. It was the opening day of hunting season.

"How'd ya sleep?"

"Ahh, not too well; I think I was a bit excited."

"That's usually the case," my dad said with a grin, transferring two fried eggs, an elk sausage patty, hashbrowns and toast to my plate. "Why don't you lead us in a prayer before we dig in."

"Lord, we thank you for this special day, and ask that You keep us safe, and make our shots true. Amen."

"Amen; thanks, Son."

"Where will we be hunting today?" I asked cutting into my sausage with my fork.

"I think we'll ride up to Grouse Gulch this morning. We'll need to be in the saddle by 6:30, so we'll get there at daylight," he said dipping his toast into one of his egg yolks. "Hopefully, we'll catch some elk out grazing...if not, there's a good chance a few will head that way when the shootin' starts over in the Tyler Creek area," he added starting on his second egg and second piece of toast.

I hadn't even finished my first few bites. My dad could eat faster than anyone I've ever known."

"After breakfast, if you clean up the dishes and make us a couple of lunches, I'll start saddling up the horses," he added washing down the last of his breakfast with his orange juice.

"Okay, sounds good" I said attempting to eat faster even though not quite awake yet.

"How far is it from your ranch to Grouse Gulch?" Nick asked as they entered their barracks.

"About a mile and a half as the crow flies, but probably more like three miles on the trails we have to take to get up there. It's a steady, difficult climb for the horses—takes them about 1 1/2 hours to reach Bobcat Pass that leads into Grouse Gulch."

"Did you see any elk on the ride up?"

"Not a one, and none at Grouse either. It was getting to be shooting light, so we began to hear a few gunshots from hunters over in the Tyler Creek area to the west of us. We hung out in the Pass for awhile above the Gulch, glassing the terrain with our binoculars, just in case any elk had been pushed our way. When none appeared, my dad suggested we continue riding over a ridge to the south side of Grouse Gulch."

"Any elk that are in here will be bedding down by now," my dad said dismounting. He led his horse over to a grouping of small firs. "Let's tie up our horses here and put our orange vests over our saddle horns just in case there happens to be another hunter in this area. Okay, give me about a hundred yard lead; then follow me across this slope about 75 yards lower than I am. The elk like to lie on benches facing downhill, so really watch below for any movement. If you hear me shoot, get ready in case any elk head your way. I'll do the same. If we haven't seen anything by the time we get to the next gulch, we'll head back to our horses."

"Okay," I nodded. I was both excited, yet a bit nervous because going for your first elk was a big deal in our family.

"Did you guys see any elk bedded down?" Nick asked as they got their gear in order and prepared to get a few hours of shut eye before reporting back for the final briefing.

"No, but after my dad had walked about 100 yards, I heard him yell something about a bear."

"What!?" I shouted back. I could see my dad looking down at something with his rifle at-the-ready, so I ran toward him. "Did you say something about a bear?"

"Yes!" he replied pointing to a small opening below a big rock that jutted out of the hillside. "As I walked past here, I saw a bear stick its head out of this hole; when he saw me, he retreated back in there."

"Oh my gosh—he was *really* close to your leg!"

"I *know*! I couldn't believe it!"

Our main goal that day was to get me an elk, so I asked him what he was going to do.

"Try to shoot it!" he said. "I've got my bear tag...won't ever get luckier than this! Do you have your little flashlight handy?"

"Yes," I replied. I removed my fanny pack, unzipped the front pouch, removed the flashlight and handed it to my dad.

My dad turned it on and crouching down, pointed it into the opening.

"See anything?" I asked.

"Not really...looks like it goes back a ways and slants downward.... Oh...wait...I can see his eyes now, glowing back at me from the flashlight. Okay, let me get his position in my mind. I'm guessing he's eight to ten feet back in there." He handed the flashlight back to me and told me to stand back. "I'm going to shoot a few rounds in there." He positioned the barrel of his .30 .06 into the opening and slightly downward. **BOOM!** The loud bang was oddly muffled—like the loud, dull thud an M-80 firecracker makes when it explodes under a bucket. He ejected the shell, then, slightly changing the angle of the barrel, fired again. **BOOM!** After his fourth shot, he handed me his rifle, took mine and fired all four of my 7mm .08 shells into the cave, each at a slightly different angle. He gave my rifle back to me, turned my flashlight back on and shined it into the opening again. "Okay, I can't see its eyes anymore and it's motionless. I think he's dead," he added standing up and turning off the flashlight.

"How are you going to get it out of there?" I asked looking at the small opening.

"We'll have to pull it out of there with a rope and one of our horses. Can you go back and get our horses?"

"Sure...back in a jiff," I said leaving my rifle and gear there.

"Did you have any idea he'd ask you to go into the bear's den?" Nick asked.

I shook my head. "Not until I brought the horses back."

My dad reloaded his rifle and placed it nearby where he could reach it easily. "Hand me the rope from my saddle, son.... Now...there's no way my body's going to fit through that small opening, so you're going to have to go in with your flashlight and tie the rope about the bear's neck," he said, unraveling the rope. "You can follow the rope back to the opening."

"But, Dad...we don't know the bear's dead for sure," I exclaimed. "What if it isn't?"

"I'll tie this rope around your waist; if the bear's still alive, just let me know and I'll pull you out. You'll probably have to take off your hunting jacket to fit through there."

"Dad...I don't know...I...."

"You can do this, Son. I could see some blood on the bear when I shined the flashlight on it, and it didn't move at all."

I slowly and reluctantly removed my coat, not at all sure about this. I watched my dad tie a slip knot, make a loop and put it around my waist. We locked eyes for a second, then he nodded at me. I looked down, knelt in front of the hole, turned on my flashlight and peered into the hole as far as I could. Then, I cautiously stuck my head into the opening. I was able to get my torso through the opening, but the pockets of my Army fatigue pants were full of stuff and kept me from going farther into the opening. I backed out.

"I'm going to have to take these off to get through," I said, "which means I'm going to have to remove my boots too." I was shaking.

"Okay," my dad said. His voice was calm and assuring.

I unlaced my hunting boots, pulled them off, but kept my socks on. I unbuckled my pants and removed them. "Alright, I'll try to get through now," I said. Dressed only in my long johns and socks, and the rope around my waist, I was now able to get my torso and the rest of my body through the small opening. Once I was about three feet into the cave, I could smell the cave's dankness and another really foul odor. I panicked! "Dad...pull me out!" I shouted. My dad quickly pulled me back to the opening.

"What's wrong, Son...is it still alive?"

"I don't know...Dad, I'm just scared...I don't think I can do this...."

"Listen, Son. You can do this! *You* are the only one who can control your fear. Tell you what. Let's say a prayer together, so you will be able to overcome your fear. This will be a life-changing moment for you."

I knew I wouldn't be able to change my dad's mind, so I bowed my head and closed my eyes tight. "Lord, please help me overcome my fear so I can go in and tie the rope around the bear's head, so we can pull it out...and please protect me."

My dad put his hand on my shoulder and said, "Good job, Son. You got this."

I guess, even though I was scared spitless, I just determined I had to go in there. So, carrying the small flashlight in my left hand, I wriggled through the opening again.

"Is the bear still in the same position?" my dad asked.

"Yes...I think it's dead."

"Can you see how far the den goes back?"

"Ahh, I think maybe about ten feet. Man, it really stinks in here!"

"Okay, Son...I'll give you some slack in the rope so you can release the loop from around your waist, then slip it over the bear's head and cinch it tight. When you're done, turn around and follow the rope out. I'll have a tight hold of it."

I positioned the flashlight so I could see the bear's head. I could see blood on its head and face and felt more confident that it was dead. After I placed the loop around the bear's neck and cinched it tight, I turned around and began crawling toward the opening. I tried really hard to not think about the bear reaching out to grab my leg as I crawled toward the opening.

When I stuck my head through the opening, I felt a huge sense of relief and pride that I'd accomplished this fearsome task. I squinted as my eyes adjusted to the daylight, but I could see that my dad was smiling broadly at me.

"Nice job, Son!" he said giving me a big hug. "I'm so proud of you!"

"Thanks," I replied smiling but still shaking.

"Go ahead and get your clothes on; then we'll pull your bear out."

"But Dad, it's *your* bear," I said. "You're the one who discovered it and shot it."

"But, *you're* the one who entered the den to go get it. You're the real hero here, Son. No, this bear is *yours*, and every time you look at its hide, you'll remember this special life event."

"Was it difficult to get the bear out?" Nick asked as they prepared to hit the sack.

"Not really. Once my dad's horse began to pull, it pretty much came right out. First its bloody head. The horse had to strain a bit to get its shoulders through, but the bear's body just seemed to adjust to the small opening as it was pulled out. Then, the hind quarters. Some of the bear's fur did get left behind on the rocky entrance."

"Did you and your dad skin it out there?"

"Yes. After field dressing it, we removed the fur, including the head, 'cause my dad wanted to get a full rug made of it.

"Oh, you'll love this! As we're skinning it, my dad said, 'One more thing, Son...promise me you won't tell Mom about this. If you do, I'll never hear the end of it.'"

"Okay," I said nodding my head.

"Did she ever find out?"

"Yeah, she saw my long johns when I was putting them in the washer and asked how in the devil they got so dirty. So, I ended up telling her."

"Did your dad get into trouble?"

"Oh, yeah! All I heard her yell from the front room was, 'How could you ask your own son to do that....!?' I'm sure there was more said, because they went out onto the front porch. But, after that, everything kind of returned to normal. I'm sure deep down, my mom was proud of me as well."

"Did you get an elk on the way back to the ranch?" Nick asked laying down on his bunk.

"No, but I wasn't really disappointed. Working up the courage to go in that cave and pulling it out of there was plenty of excitement for one day. And, I knew my dad would help me find an elk before the end of the season."

"I can certainly understand how this memory helps you deal with the anxiety and fear that comes with these missions," Nick said. "Maybe it will help me deal with my fears as well."

John glanced at Nick, nodded, then rolled over. He let the vivid images of that bear experience with his dad flow through his mind until he fell asleep.

Nick did his best to imagine what it must have been like for John to crawl into that cave, not knowing if the bear was dead or alive....

"Okay, men. As you know, this is an important mission for us," said the CO after reviewing recon updates and roles. "God speed! We will debrief after you return. Dismissed!"

John and Nick headed for their idling bus. It would take them to the airfield, where a CH-47 Chinook was warming to transport them over the rugged Afghan terrain to their target. Adjusting his gear, John grinned at Nick, "Let's go get us a bear!"

First Bull

B uck reined Jewel to an abrupt halt. "***Elk!***" Buck yelled, quickly pointing toward the open area below us....

The last time I'd hunted with Buck Wiley was in the fall of 1973, some 27 years ago when we taught and coached together in Eastern Washington. When I called Buck to inform him that I'd just retired from my principal position in Washington State, he said, "Okay, no more excuses about being 'too busy' to come over and hunt. You're coming over this fall; you can use one of our rifles and ride one of our horses."

"Okay, I'll be there."

"Brady!" Buck yelled as I entered the main terminal lobby after disembarking on Tuesday, October 24, 2000 in Missoula. Buck, still dressed in his teaching clothes—short-sleeved shirt, slacks and no coat despite the cold temperature outside, gave me one of his trademark bear hugs.

"Are ya ready to kill somethin'?" he asked with a big smile.

"Yes! Let's head for the ranch!"

Buck effortlessly tossed my big, heavy *American Tourister* suitcase, loaded with all my hunting gear, into the back of his old Chevy pick-up. His 6'1" frame was all muscle. He possessed that indisputable strength that comes from working on a horse ranch: bucking bales, installing fence posts, mending fence wire, breaking horses and hunting elk.

During the 40 mile drive from the airport to the ranch, east of Missoula, we caught up on family news, and Buck gave me a run down on tomorrow's hunt. "You'll be ridin' Ivan—you've ridden him before when you've been here in the summers."

"Yes! He's such a well-trained horse—I appreciate it!"

"After we get to the ranch, we'll get all our stuff organized for the morning; then I'll put a saddle on Ivan so it's all adjusted for you. We want to head out before daylight so we can be near Bobcat Pass just as it's starting to get light. Hopefully, we'll jump some elk in that area."

"Sounds great, Buck! I'm so looking forward to hunting with you again!" I'd ridden through Bobcat Pass with Buck during the summers when our family had visited the Wileys, and had seen the elk campsite at Grouse Gultch. But it was always dismantled; not set up for hunting.

"Man! Looks like you, Leah and the kids have done some more remodeling since the last time I was here," I said setting my suitcase down in the foyer of the ranch house.

"Yes, Brady—just for you!" he chuckled setting my hunting boots on the floor. "Put your stuff in Jamie's room upstairs; it's probably the cleanest in the place." This was good news to me because her bedroom was on the south side of the house, farthest from the interstate and the railroad tracks. I knew from visiting the ranch during the summers, that the traffic noise on I-90 and the freight trains that rumble by on a fairly regular basis are much louder from guest rooms on the north side.

"I'll get a fire goin' while you're organizing the stuff you want to wear and take hunting tomorrow," Buck yelled from the living room. "When you come down, I'll show you the rifle you'll be using, and get you some shells."

When I got downstairs, Buck closed the squeeky door to the wood stove and handed me a short-barreled rifle. "Okay, you'll be usin'

Jeff's 7mm .08. It's all sighted in, so all you have to do is hold it steady when you pull the trigger. Here's how you load it—just press three shells into the magazine one by one like this," he demonstrated. "And, here's another shell to keep in the pocket of your hunting pants. Once we start hunting tomorrow, load one shell into the chamber; then add the shell from your pocket into the magazine like this...so you'll have *four* shots instead of three. Always reload after you've taken some shots, so you'll have as many shots as possible in your rifle," he said, unloading the chamber and magazine and handing the shells to me.

I practiced loading the ammo a couple of times. "Okay, got it."

"Well, before it gets too dark, let's go out to the corral and get your saddle set up so we don't have to do that tomorrow morning."

We talked more about family during dinner, then started watching a movie on TV. It wasn't long before our full tummies and the cozy warmth emanating from the wood stove caused both of us to yawn.

"Thanks for dinner, Buck and for getting the horses ready for tomorrow morning. What time are you going to get up?"

"Probably about a quarter 'til 5:00. I'll go out and feed our horses; then wake you about 5:15. Good night, B; don't let the bears bite."

"G'night, Buck; see you in the morning."

I lay in bed trying to control my excitement about tomorrow's hunt so I could get to sleep. In the distance, I could hear the whir of tires from intermittent vehicles crossing the overpass at the Bearmouth exit. Then came the blare of a freight train horn announcing its approach from the west. I listened to the rhythmic click-clack of the cars as they rolled by just north of us near the frontage road...then the fading *long-short-long* horn blasts farther east after the last rail car passed. *Why does a distant train horn always sound so lonely?*

The next thing I knew, I was reaching for the bedside table to silence the persistent beeping of my digital watch. I depressed the illumination button and had to blink several times before I could clearly read the 5:00 am display. *It's time! Time to get ready to hunt!* After slipping out from under the warm covers, I hurried into my long underwear and flannel shirt because the room felt really cold. *The fire definitely went out over night.* Buck, who must have already been out to feed and water the horses, was now rummaging around the kitchen. "Mornin', B! Are eggs, elk sausage and toast okay with you?"

"Sounds good," I replied sleepily, heading for the downstair's bathroom to pee and wash my face.

"Make yourself some coffee if you want."

"Thank you, I'll need it!"

After dishing up at the stove, we sat down at the kitchen table, and Buck reviewed the route we'd be taking once we left the ranch. "We'll head up a draw that continues up the hill past Medicine Hill. From there we'll climb a steep grade up to a logging road near Bobcat Pass. This area typically has quite a few Whitetail, so if you see something, get off your horse as fast as you can, hand me your reins, grab your rifle and shoot. They're only going to give you a few seconds to shoot before they take off."

"Okay," I replied with nervous excitement.

Buck finished his meal well before I did and carried his plate over to the sink. "If you wouldn't mind takin' care of the dishes and makin' us each a sandwich after you finish, I'll go out and start gettin' the horses ready. There's lunch meat and apples in the fridge, and some candy bars in the pantry. When you're ready to go, just start bringing out what you want to take and we'll load up and make tracks outta here. Oh, and could you please bring out the two meat sacks by the front door?"

"Will do," I answered washing down the last of my breakfast with a gulp of coffee.

I placed the 7mm .08, our lunches, the meat sacks, and my day-pack outside the front door, turned off the house lights and closed the door. I looked out to the spot-lit corral area where both horses were now saddled, heads down, nibbling on the last of the oats in their bowls. Buck was bringing out their bridles from the tack room.

"Here's your lunch, Buck and the meat sacks."

"Thanks, B. Go ahead and put your daypack over the saddle horn on the right side and secure it with the leather straps. Oh, and in the tack room, there's an orange pannier and two lengths of bailing twine on the floor. Could you roll up the pannier, secure it with the twine, then tie it to the back of your saddle with the saddle straps. I've got one on the back of my saddle too. If we both get an elk, we're gonna need both of these panniers."

"Got it."

While I was tying the pannier to the back of my saddle, Buck picked up the horses' bowls, and began putting on their bridles.

"Okay, before heading out, load a shell into your chamber, then add the extra shell to your magazine." My hands were shaking a bit as I did so. I couldn't tell if it was due to my excitement or the chilly morning air. "Make sure your safety's on, then put your rifle into your scabbard.... Okay, B, why don't you get on Ivan before I turn off the lights."

I placed my left boot in the stirrup on Ivan's left side, grabbed the reins and his withers with my left hand and swung my right leg over the saddle. I felt like I was a loooong way from the ground.

When Buck turned out the bright spot lights that lit up the corral area and hitching posts, I understood why he wanted me to mount first. Suddenly, it was *pitch dark*! I couldn't see *a thing*. It took several seconds for my eyes to adjust enough to see Buck's shadowy figure leading Jewel out the gate. Squeezing with my legs, I signaled Ivan to follow.

Once on the driveway next to the ranch house, Buck threw a leg over Jewel and headed past the wood pile toward a draw. To my surprise, Ivan broke into a trot to catch up with Jewel.

"Ah, he's ready to move out, huh," Buck chuckled. "Let's see if he's that enthusiastic after we start the climb to Bobcat Pass."

It amazed me how the horses could see where they were going up the narrow, uneven, *very dark* gulch. Every once in awhile, I could see sparks from Jewel's shoes as they struck rocks on the trail. As we climbed, the horses passed gas loudly, and at times, I could hear them dropping a few "road apples."

Buck looked back and chuckled. "Healthy puppies aren't they!"

When we reached the south fence line, Buck dismounted and released the wire loop holding the barbed wire gate closed. Once Ivan and I were through the opening, he pulled the gate across the opening, reattached the wire loop and remounted.

"Thanks, Buck; I'll get it on the way back," I chuckled.

We continued walking south up a narrow trail through low growing shrubs and short, bushy pines that brushed against our legs as we rode through them.

"That's called 'Medicine Hill'," Buck informed me as we rode past a shadowy dome-shaped hill to our right. Soon, we turned directly south again heading toward the base of a steep hillside. The trail led us into a grove of Aspen trees before ascending up the steep west-facing slope. "Lean forward in the saddle," Buck instructed. "It'll make it easier for Ivan to climb."

Now the horses were really laboring, and I understood why their tack included chest straps to keep the saddles from sliding backwards. After about 200 yards, we rested our horses on yet another logging road that cut across the west-facing hillside. The horses panted heavily and Buck dismounted, signaling me to do the same. "We'll give them a breather for a bit before heading on up," Buck said stepping away from Jewel to pee. After finishing, he added, "Let's tighten our cinches; they've no doubt loosened up a bit by now."

After remounting, we urged our horses upward, zigzagging back and forth across the hillside to ease the steady climb a bit for the horses. Ivan and Jewel enjoyed two more rests before they carried us to a ridge below Bobcat Pass. The eastern sky was beginning to lighten now, so we peered down into the steep drainage to the east of us to look for movement.

"I don't see anything," Buck whispered as the horses breathed heavily expelling steam from their noses. "It's amazing the distance these horses have covered in such a short time. Can you imagine how tired and sweaty we'd be if we tried walking up here carrying our rifles and gear!?" Buck looked up the next slope. "They have one more steep climb through these trees before they hit the logging road."

Finally, after a couple more brief rests, the horses lunged up onto a logging road that ran east and west; Buck urged Jewel east. "Onward to Bobcat Pass, Brady."

It felt colder up here, and I wished I was wearing yet another layer.

Buck motioned for me to ride up next to him. "Watch the area to your right as we ride up the road; I'll watch the area to my left. If you spot a deer or elk, get off as quickly as you can and hand me your reins, okay?"

I nodded.

After walking the horses about a half mile, Buck stopped and whispered to me, "I'm not seeing any fresh tracks; let's lope these guys a ways to get to the top while it's still getting light."

I managed to push my hat down farther before Ivan broke into a trot to keep up with Jewel. Trotting the horses always made me nervous as I had difficulty staying square in the saddle. I tried my best to stand up a bit in the stirrups so the saddle wouldn't beat me up, but I found it difficult to maintain my balance. I was relieved when Buck slowed Jewel to a walk again as we approached the top of a rise that merged with another logging road coming in from our right.

"This is the north end of Bobcat Pass," Buck pointed out. "The road straight ahead of us will take us to Grouse Gulch where the camp is. Keep your eyes peeled; I've shot a lot of deer and some elk in this area."

The cold breeze blowing through this open area made both of

us tie our ear flaps under our chins. To our right was the beginning of a rocky, rugged butte comprised of jagged reddish-colored bluffs and gnarly bushes. It reminded me of scenes from western movies I'd watched as a kid. This section of road contained more rocks due to the rugged terrain it paralleled, and the horses' shoes *clip-clopped* against them as they walked. Buck and I used our cow calls to keep any elk that might be in the area from being frightened away by the horses. To the left of the road, the terrain dropped down into a more open area dotted with occasional fir trees. I took a deep breath and thanked God for giving me this opportunity to ride through such beautiful wilderness.

Ahead of us, the logging road split. I knew from riding with Buck during the summer that the road to the left veered down toward Grouse Gulch, where the elk camp was, and where we'd be spending tonight.

"No elk here this morning," Buck said, urging Jewell right.

After a short ride, we rode into a wide clearing and Buck stopped.

"We call this 'Grouse Saddle'. Ya know that big seven point elk rack on the living room wall?"

I nodded.

"I shot him one morning when I had just entered this 'saddle' from Bobcat Pass." Buck pointed to the top of the ridge just south of us. "He was standing up there in the trees. It was kind of foggy, and steam was coming out of his nose and rising from his body. I got off my horse, got my rifle, aimed and shot. He took off and I thought I'd missed him. I jumped back on my horse and ran up that trail to where he'd been standin'. I could see where he'd pivoted and taken off so I followed his tracks. Well, he'd run about 75 yards and fallen dead. I'd hit him in the neck. It was a mighty lucky shot because he was in the trees, surrounded by fog and steam. I could have easily hit one of the trees he was standing by."

I listened intently taking in every detail. "Is that the biggest elk you've ever shot?"

"By far. He was a real monster!" Buck added staring up at the ridge—like he was reliving that epic moment in his mind.... "Okay, we're going to ride up that trail and follow the ridge line until we come out into a second saddle that we call Moyle Saddle. Keep your eyes peeled for elk; they could very well be feeding or bedded down between here and there. You scope out the right side of the trail; I'll scope out the left side."

"Okay," I nodded. "Just don't lose me 'cause I wouldn't have any idea how to get back to the ranch."

This wispy trail followed the spine of a rocky ridge that dropped off sharply on each side. I would have been more at ease leading Ivan on foot, rather than riding him. Both slopes were dark from the dense trees that hemmed them in. I scanned the trees carefully as we rode across the spine, expecting to spot an elk at any moment. I was so hopeful...but nothing. A steep descent down into a clearing greeted us at the edge of the ridge.

"Let's dismount here and lead our horses down," Buck directed. Hunting boots sideways into the gravely, rocky slope to keep from sliding, he led Jewel carefully down toward the clearing. After allowing them some distance, I did the same.

"Here we are, B—Moyle Saddle. If we ever split up and I say, 'Let's meet in Moyle Saddle', this is where we'd meet." I looked about attempting to lock in some landmarks. "The continuing trail across the way will lead us into Moyle Gulch," Buck said pointing south. As you'll see, it's almost like a hidden passage into a whole different climate zone. You'll be amazed!"

The trail we followed up the next ridge looked very similar to the one we'd just been on, only when we came to its end, an open, nearly treeless hillside greeted us. We traversed this open slope for quite a distance until we came to a well-used game trail that led down toward a line of dense woods. The abrupt contrast in terrain made the trail at that point look like it was leading into a dark cave. As we entered, morning daylight suddenly changed to shadowed afternoon light. The density of the lodgepole pine was dramatic. *No wonder it's so much darker in here!* In a short distance, the trail crossed a slide area of large black boulders.

"Just your toes in the stirrups, Brady," Buck cautioned. "If your horse should trip, be ready to bail outta your saddle into the hillside. Do *not* roll down the hill with the horse!"

Oh, my God! I thought, looking left down the steep slope covered by large jagged boulders. I made sure my toes were just barely in the stirrups, and I placed my left palm on top of the saddle horn so I could push myself upward and off Ivan's back to my right if I had to bail. Once we crossed the slide, I patted Ivan on the neck, relieved. "Good boy!"

The game trail descended gradually downward and then flattened out a bit. Soon, it crossed a small narrow streamlet that seemed to originate right out of the hillside. I looked for its source up the hillside but there was none. *That's strange!* Buck urged Jewel across it first. "Make sure Ivan *walks* across it," emphasized Buck. "Don't let him jump it."

After Ivan walked across the streamlet, we began to climb gradually, and as we did so, I was once again taken by how dense the trees were and how lush the undergrowth was. *Buck's right—it's like a completely different climate zone in here!* The trees were tall and skinny; the grass on the forest floor green, thick and bushy. As the trail bent to the left, Buck directed Jewel to his right away from the trail. The horses' hooves made a *swish, swish* sound as they walked through the thick grass.

As we rode, I began to notice the blazes that someone had made on the trees. *Probably Buck*, I thought as he seemed to be following them.

After riding through the trees for about twenty minutes, Buck stopped and turned back toward me and whispered, "Get off here, B and give me your reins. Take your rifle and walk ahead of me. I'll give you about a 100 yard lead. I've shot a few elk in here. Walk real slow, looking ahead through the trees, and carefully scan all sides for any movement. The elk are bedded down this time of day so are hard to see unless you can spot some movement that gives them away."

I walked slowly ahead as Buck had coached. At one point, I glanced back just to make sure I could still see him and the horses. *Shit, I'd be screwed if something happened to Buck; I have no idea where I'm at!* Then, about 75 yards in front of me, I saw something black move. *Shit, a bear!* I got behind a tree to keep hidden and to use it to steady my aim in case I had to shoot it. I slowly peaked around the tree. So far, It hadn't seen or smelled me. Its head was down in the brush and it looked like it was eating. Suddenly, it lifted its head. *It's a cow moose! I wonder if Buck would want me to shoot it?* Then, I saw another movement behind the cow—her calf! *That answers that; there's no way I'm going to shoot the cow and leave the calf an orphan.* About that time, I could hear the horses approaching, and so did the cow. She made a "bark-like" noise. The calf fled into the forest and the cow followed. I motioned for Buck to come quickly. "Oh my God, Buck! There was a cow moose with her calf, right over there!" I said excitedly. About that time, a loud bellow echoed through the forest.

"That's the cow," Buck said. "She wants us to leave. Go ahead and remount; we'll ride a bit farther then circle back." The bellows continued as we rode. It was as if the cow and her calf were keeping track of us, but just far enough away to stay hidden. The intermittent bellowing continued until we had turned around and were well out of the cow's domain.

After riding for about 15 minutes, I could see from the trampled grass we were returning the same way we'd ridden in. When we reached the main trail, Buck stopped and motioned for me to ride up next to him.

"I wanted to show you the trapper's cabin today, Brady, but given the time of day, I think we'll save that for another day and head back toward Grouse. By the time we eat our lunches and make a pass through Grouse, it'll be late afternoon and time to head down to the elk camp. If we should run into some elk, we could very well be ridin' down there in the dark."

As we rode back north toward Grouse, we crossed the streamlet again, which reminded me that we'd once again have to cross the rock slide. My gut twitched. As we approached it, I made sure only my toes were in the stirrups; this time, I placed my *right* palm on the saddle horn in case I'd have to launch myself left into the rocky hillside. *Not a good option, but better than rolling down the rock slide with my horse.* At one point in this precarious crossing, our horses had to step up about a foot and a half to a natural stair-step in the trail. I held my breath. When Ivan had successfully reached the end of the slide area, I breathed a sigh of relief and patted him on the neck.

Once again, I was struck by the significant difference in light when we emerged from the dense forest into the exposed hillside. When we reached the opening at Moyle Saddle, we were harshly greeted by the chilly breeze out of the north.

"Given how cold it is, Brady, let's ride down to a game trail rather than back up to the exposed ridge we came over. This route will get us out of this cold wind."

I quickly nodded, and Buck directed Jewel to his right down a fairly steep hillside. Immediately, we were out of the direct wind and much warmer. After about a 10 minute ride, Buck headed down to another, less traveled game trail that brought us into a peaceful clearing surrounded by huge, colorful Ponderosa pines.

"Let's stop here and eat our lunches before heading back up to Grouse Saddle," Buck said.

"Should we tie up the horses, Buck?"

"Naw...we'll let them feed a bit on some grass while we eat; we won't be here long."

It felt good to get out of the saddle for a bit, sit on the soft grass and enjoy our deli sandwiches. Our horses seemed to enjoy the break as well, tearing off mouthfuls of grass and chewing away.

"One time, Jeff, John and I stopped here to eat our lunches—just like we are—and a small herd of about six elk migrated by, about 100 yards just east of us," Buck said pointing. "We sprinted for our rifles, started blasting away, and were able to down two of them."

"Oh, that we'd be so lucky again," I said finishing my sandwich and taking the apple out of my daypack.

After we finished our apples, we fed the cores to our horses, remounted and continued north on the trail. When the trail split, Buck chose the upward route. "This will take us up to Grouse Saddle," Buck said.

When we rode over the top of the hill and into Grouse Saddle, we were once again in direct contact with the cold north wind. "Brrrr, that wind is cold!!" said Buck turning toward me in his saddle and fastening his ear flaps. "Tell ya what, Brady...let's head over to the west side of this outcropping. This branch of the logging road eventually wraps around to the other side of Bobcat Pass—maybe we'll spot an elk down in the canyon."

"Okay, sounds good to me," I responded, fastening my ear flaps as well, and making sure the zipper to my jacket was up all the way. I wished I'd brought some type of windbreaker to wear over my wool jacket, for we'd now be riding head on into the frigid wind.

The left edge of the road dropped off sharply into a deep canyon. *Holy shit! It would be crazy to shoot an elk down there—how would we even get down to it?* While I wanted to get an elk, I was silently hoping we wouldn't spot one while riding the length of this road. Fortunately, given the cold wind and time of day, we did not.

At the north end of the rugged butte where the road curved to the east, back toward Bobcat Pass, Buck stopped to scan the canyon again. He was hunched down as far as he could into his jacket. His face was red from the cold wind. It was about 3:00 pm and daylight was beginning to fade under the graying skies.

"No elk down there," he shouted. "Let's lope the horses over to the Pass, Brady; hopefully we'll run into some elk on the other side."

It must feel good to the horses to run for a bit in this cold, I thought. *Can't wait to get out of this chilly wind and light a fire in the stove at the elk camp...*

"**Elk!**" Buck yelled, quickly pointing toward the open area below us. "Grab your rifle and hang on to your reins!" he shouted dismounting and pulling his rifle out of his scabbard. I reined-in Ivan, blinking to clear my watery eyes. I took my cues from Buck, who led Jewel to the edge of the road and stepped on her reins with his right foot. I could see them now—two young bulls down at the far end of the logged-out area below us—about 200 yards away. The bulls hadn't yet spotted us or caught our scent thanks to the wind.

"You take the one on the right; I'll take the one on the left. Ready—one, two, thr...Buck's rifle roared first; then mine. **BOOM... BOOM**! The two bulls lifted their heads and began to run back and forth across the far end of the clearing as if confused. "Keep shootin'!" Buck yelled. I placed the crosshairs on my moving elk and fired again. **BOOM**! "Don't let them run outta there!" Buck shot two more times and shouted, "Mine's down; keep firing at yours."

I couldn't tell if I'd hit my elk, which was now heading up out of the open area toward an embankment to our right. Buck shot his last bullet at my retreating bull but it continued its escape route up the treed slope.

"Quick—run up the road and head him off...I've got your horse. Take another shot before he heads over the top!"

I sprinted up the logging road with my rifle until I could see the bull emerging through the trees. My heart was pounding due to the adrenaline rush and my sprint up the road. I took a knee in an attempt to steady my aim, tried my best to slow my breathing, placed the cross hairs on the elk, held my breath and fired—**BOOM**! *Please go down!* But the frantic bull disappeared over the top of the slope.

"*Brady!*" Buck yelled from below. "Come back down, get on Ivan and head over there to see if he's down!"

I jogged back down the road to where Buck was holding Ivan, and started to return my rifle to the scabbard.

"Before you do that, reload! You might get another shot at him." I released my ammo holder and reloaded with shaking hands. "Good. Okay...saddle up and head over there. I'll ride down and gut out my bull, then come over and help you look."

Ivan was reluctant to charge up the road. He kept looking back toward Buck and Jewel, who were heading down into the clearing.

"Ivan, this way!" I urged kicking him with my heels. He obeyed, but kept looking to his left and snorting. "It's okay, Ivan, they'll join us in a bit," I said trying to calm his fears. I trotted Ivan up the road about 200 yards; then reined him left off the road to the top of the slope where I'd last seen the fleeing bull. "There's where he came over, Ivan," I said aloud looking at the fresh tracks that led up to the top and over. Ivan looked back to his left again to where Buck and Jewel were below us. "Ivan, walk!" I commanded urging him to follow the elk's tracks down the other side. I looked for any sign of blood, but found none. *Shit, I don't think I hit him....* It was turning dusk and getting difficult to follow the elk's tracks. *There are so many different elk tracks on this slope....* I reined Ivan to the right across the hillside for a ways; then farther down the slope and to the left—zigzagging back and forth. *Not much daylight left,* I thought hoping to see some evidence that the bull was wounded. By now, it was almost dark.

"Any luck?" shouted Buck from the top of the slope.

"No, and I don't see any blood."

Ivan whinnied as if relieved to see Jewel and Buck, who walked down toward us in a zigzag pattern.

"Well, we'd better head down to the camp before it gets totally dark," Buck said when he reached me and Ivan. "We'll come back tomorrow morning and look when there's more light."

"Damn! Sorry, Buck."

"You may have hit him, B; don't give up hope. Elk can run a long ways after they've been hit. I've got my elk propped open with a branch; he'll be fine until tomorrow given how cold it is."

During the ride down to the camp, I felt so disappointed, and that I'd let Buck down, and that I'd missed a golden opportunity to get my first bull. When we arrived at the stream bed in the canyon, Buck stopped and gave Jewel some rein. "Let's let 'em drink before we cross the bridge."

After the horses had drunk their fill, we led them to a narrow, man-made wooden bridge straddling the creek. I was surprised at how willing the horses were to be led across such a narrow bridge.

They've obviously done this before. We led them over to the rear of the shelter. We removed our rifles and hung them by their straps under the tarp on nails protruding from the A-frame supports. "If we take our rifles inside, the scopes will fog up when we bring them outside in the morning," Buck explained.

We removed our saddles and hung them over wooden supports constructed underneath the plastic overhang. We next placed the saddle blankets on top of the saddles upside down. "They'll dry out better this way," Buck noted. The reins were hung behind the saddles on nails driven part way into one of the framing poles. Using our lead ropes, we led the horses to the corral just southwest of the tent and slid the lodgepole gate across its entrance. Buck handed me a bucket. "If you'll fill this from the stream and put it in the corral, I'll get them some grub from inside."

By the time I had filled the bucket and was heading toward the tent, Buck had lit a propane lantern. He then filled two large cardboard trays with feed pellets that were stored inside the tent in a metal garbage can, and slid the trays under the lowest corral pole so the horses could reach the pellets. "Now, we can get a fire goin' and think about some dinner," Buck said heading back toward the shelter. "Let's each take in an armload of wood."

Once inside the shelter, Buck pointed to the corner by the wood stove. "If you'll roll up some of that paper, put some of the kindling on top with a few smaller logs, I'll show you how I get this baby goin'."

As soon as I was finished preparing the stove, Buck took a small flare from a box, removed its cap, and struck the end of the flare with the gritty end of the cap. It ignited with a *pop*, and he placed it inside the kindling. "I get these from a guy who works for the railroad; best fire starters by far!" Within minutes, a dull roar could be heard inside the stove. "You won't believe how toasty we'll be in awhile, B. Just keep stokin' it. If you want to hang up your coat or anything else, just use one of the nails above the bunks. And, if you'll be so kind as to unroll the mattress pads and sleeping bags, I'll start gettin' some grub together." He grabbed two cans of food from the make-shift counter along the west side of the tent. "Tonight, on the menu, we have canned chili or canned ravioli; which would you prefer?"

"Hmmm, such a difficult decision...how about...*ravioli*?"

"Darn! I was hoping for chili," Buck laughed. "No, I'm just kidding. ravioli it is!"

It didn't take long for the fire, now raging in the wood stove, to heat up our small enclosure. I had to remove my coat and flannel shirt even before I was done unrolling the sleeping pads and bags.

"See what I mean about it getting toasty," Buck smiled stirring the ravioli in the pan atop the wood stove.

By the time dinner was served, we were both clad only in our long underwear. As we ate, Buck explained how he and his sons, Jeff and John had put the camp together over several years, and how long they'd been using it. He also shared some of their hunting stories while staying back here.

"Do you have to carry in all your supplies and equipment every year?"

"No, we have a locked, bear-proof metal box out back that's framed in with logs. It holds things like the utensils, pots and pans, lanterns, the stove, tarp, etc. It's pretty well hidden—you'd almost have to know where it is to find it. I'll show it to you sometime."

"Have bears ever tried to get in it?"

"Oh yeah! In fact, one time, one broke through the wood frame and tried to tear through the metal box. You can see where it bit clean through the sheet metal; it had to be a pretty good-sized bear!"

Now I really hope I don't have to 'go' during the middle of the night, I thought as I ate my ravioli.

When we were finished with the dishes, Buck yawned. "Well, I'm going to brush my teeth, take a pee, check the horses; then hit the sack. Mornin'll be here before you know it."

"What time should we get up?" I asked. "I can set the alarm on my watch."

"Oh...probably about 5:30," Buck estimated. "That'll give us time to get the stove goin', feed the horses, eat some breakfast, close things down and saddle up. First thing we'll do on our way out is see if we can find your elk."

"Man, look at all those stars!" I exclaimed looking up through the trees when we went outside. "You just don't see stars like this when you're anywhere near a city."

After brushing our teeth and peeing, we re-entered the tent, zipped up the front flaps and prepared to hit the sack. Buck stoked the stove one more time. I double checked my alarm setting and made sure my bear spray and flashlight were within easy reach before slipping into my sleeping bag. *Think I'll leave it unzipped for a bit; it's so damned hot in here now.*

"If you're all set, I'll turn out the lantern," Buck said. "Sleep tight; don't let the bears bite."

For some time, I lay there listening to the muffled pops in the wood stove as the fire consumed the logs. As usual, Buck wasted no time falling asleep. He could fall asleep faster than anyone I've ever known. The exciting events of the day danced through my mind, but the one that dominated was seeing my bull run over the top of the hill and disappear. *Sure hope we find him in the morning!*

I reached out of my sleeping bag to silence the beeping alarm on my wristwatch.

"What time is it?" Buck asked sleepily.

"Five thirty," I responded scooting back down into my sleeping bag. "Man, it's cold in here now!"

Buck chuckled. "If you turn on your flashlight, I'll light the lantern and get our fire goin'."

"Do you want me to get it, Buck?"

"Naw, I know where things are." He slipped on his moccasins and shuffled over to the shelf where he kept the matches. One flared to life and he adjusted the lantern's flame. "Let there be light!" exclaimed Buck. Then, the door to the wood stove squeaked open, newspaper was crumpled up, kindling tossed on top before adding a few small logs; then the *pop* of the igniting flare. "Heat soon," Buck assured heading back to his sleeping bag. "Think I'll stay in here 'til it warms up a bit if that's okay, B."

"Yeess," I chuckled. "Man, it cools off in a hurry when that stove isn't goin'. Think the horses would like to come in and warm up?"

"Geez, those poor critters. One night a few years ago when I was back here with the boys, it got so cold during the night that our horses would literally run around in the corral to keep warm.... Speakin' of the horses, in a few minutes, I'll get up and give 'em some food; if you'd be so kind as to get them some water again, B. And, go ahead and put some water on the stove to boil so you can make some coffee for yourself. Boil enough to use for oatmeal and washing up the dishes. After we eat, we'll close this place down, saddle up, and go look for your bull."

"Will the meat still be good if we find it, Buck?"

"Oh, yeah. Our butcher says that if you get to it within 12 hours when it's cold like it is now, it's still okay."

"Sure hope we find it...."

"Got everything?" Buck asked before leading Jewel toward the bridge.

"I think so," I replied running through a mental check list: *rifle, knife, shells, cow call, tennis shoes, day pack, orange hunting vest...*"yep."

"Well, let's go find your elk."

I looked back at the tent, its inner glow now dark. "Thanks so much for bringing me here, Buck! This is such a treat."

"You're welcome; glad you could come out this hunting season—*finally*."

The early morning daylight brightened as we rode out of the shaded Gulch back up the slope north of the camp. When we reached the area where the bull had crossed the ridge, Buck told me to ride back and forth across the hillside. "I'll ride a bit farther down this slope and see if I spot anything."

I tried to remain hopeful as I scanned the hillside for any sign of blood or fresh tracks...but nothing. *I can't believe at least one of our shots didn't hit him....* I had pretty much resigned myself to the fact that he'd escaped our shots yesterday, when I heard Buck yell from below.

"Down here, Brady! You got him!"

My spirits immediately soared and I urged Ivan down to where Buck stood. To his right lying on its left side, up against a big Ponderosa, was the dead bull. "Oh, my gosh—thank you for finding it Buck!... My first elk!" I smiled broadly.

"Good shootin', Brady!" He pointed up the hill, "Look...you can see where he bit the dust and rolled down to this tree. It'll be interesting to see where ya hit him. It's amazing how far they can run after they're hit. Grab your camera and let me get a picture of you with your first elk, B; then I'm going to pull him away from the tree a bit so we can work on him. Grab Ivan and stand by him.... There—one, two, three...."

Buck handed the camera back, tied a rope around the bull's horns, then mounting Jewel, looped the other end around the saddle horn and urged her up the slope—just enough to get the elk away from the tree with its head pointing uphill. "Looks like one of us hit him behind the shoulder. It's a little far back, but he wasn't gonna go far."

"It's probably my shot, Buck. I didn't allow for his running and lead him—I just shot."

"That's okay, Bri. You know what they say...no lead flyin'; no elk dyin'. What I try to do if they're running is put my cross hairs on the sweet spot behind their shoulder, then move it to the front a bit before firing. But, I've been huntin' these critters for a few years.

"Ya know...I think since this guy's been lyin' here awhile and is starting to smell a bit, we'll skip gutting him and just take the meat."

"How do we do that?"

"Let me have your knife and I'll show you." With the blade of my hunting knife facing upward, Buck thrust the point into the elk's hide, at the rear of the backbone to create a starting point. Then, he continued, cutting all the way up the backbone to the neck. Now, changing position, he cut through the hide from this backbone incision all the way down the rib cage behind the exposed front shoulder, being careful to not puncture the gut. He made a similar vertical cut from the backbone incision all the way down the back of the rear leg. "Okay, B, now, start from the backbone and begin separating the hide from the carcass."

When we'd removed the hide from one side, Buck asked me to get both meat sacks from my saddle bag.

"Okay, let's start with the back strap; then we'll do the quarters."

"Man, this back strap is *huge!*" I exclaimed lowering the thick, hefty, long length of muscle into the meat sack.

"And this is a young bull," Buck pointed out. "Wait 'til you see the back strap of a five or six point bull!"

After finishing one side, we placed the hide back up onto the elk and rolled it over enough to expose the other side. Buck pointed to another bullet hole in the rear quarter with his knife. "Not the best place to hit an elk, but you know what they say, B... No lead flyin', no elk dying," we chimed chuckling.

"This way is so much quicker and cleaner than removing the guts, Buck. Why don't you do this all the time?"

"Because I can sell the hides."

"Ah," I replied working to release the second back strap. "I'm guessing you won't be taking this hide in," I chuckled.

"Nope."

When both sides were done, Buck stood up and stretched out his back. "I'm not going to bother with these antlers, but you may want to take the ivories." Buck could tell by my puzzled look that I didn't understand. "Bulls have two large upper teeth that are called 'ivories'. Some think they're what allow the bulls to whistle during mating season. You may want to have them made into earrings for Patsy." Buck raised the elk's upper lip and began cutting through the gum around one of the teeth. Then, he took the butt of his knife and hit the side of the tooth until the root broke loose. "There's one," he said handing the tooth to me. I placed it in the pocket of my wool pants. "Okay, you take the other one out." I used his method but it took me a bit longer. I looked it over to make sure I hadn't broken the tooth with my knife, then placed it in my pocket.

"Now, we can load up and head for my bull." He untied the pannier from the back of Jewel's saddle, positioned it over his saddle, then led Jewel across the hillside until she was close to the meat sacks.

"You don't want Ivan to carry this?"

"Jewel's not quite as tall as Ivan, so it will be easier to put the meat sack into the pannier on this hillside."

Buck grabbed one of the full meat sacks and told me to grab the other. "Okay, you stand on the uphill side; I'll stand on the downhill side because I'm taller. On three, lift your sack and place it into the pouch. One, two, *three*...." Jewel shifted a bit to adjust to all the sudden weight placed on her back. Buck patted her on the neck, "Good girl, Jewel!

"Okay, let's exchange straps...now put my strap through the loop and cinch it up...." Buck rolled his sleeves back down, returned the rope to his saddle bag, put on his jacket, orange vest and cow call and looked around. "Always take a good look around to make sure you haven't left anything behind...okay, let's go get my elk."

We both led our horses up the hillside to the top and down into the opening where Buck's bull lay. Two large ravens and a bald eagle ascended as we neared.

"Kind of easy to tell where my elk is, isn't it?" Buck chuckled. "If you're ever looking for an animal you shot, ravens, eagles and magpies will tell you where it is, and pretty quickly after it's expired."

"Doesn't look like they've eaten much of your elk," I commented as we approached the carcass.

"That's because they've been eatin' the gut pile and the elk's eyes."

"Oh my gosh...they're both gone!" I exclaimed looking down at the bare eye sockets.

"They always go for the soft tissue first," Buck said fetching the rope again from his saddle bag. He tied one end of the rope around the bull's horns, climbed on Ivan, and, wrapping the other end around the saddle horn, gently urged Ivan forward several feet. "Now we have some room to operate....

"I want to take this hide back with us, so we won't use the same method on this guy. Let's roll him onto his back, then we can begin removing the hide. If you pull it outward, I'll separate it from the carcass."

The stiffness of the elk complicated the process a bit, but in about an hour, both meat sacks were full.

"Can I practice getting the ivories out, Buck?"

"Be my guest."

After both meat sacks were secure in Ivan's pannier, we rolled up the hide and tied it to the back of Buck's saddle.

"The bad news, B, is that we'll have to lead the horses back to the ranch because of the weight they're carrying; the good news is, walking will help us stay warm."

About halfway down the logging road that leads into Bobcat Pass, a large Mule deer doe crossed about 75 yards in front of us and stood on the left side of the road looking at us.

"What'ya think, Brady...wanna take her?"

I paused for a few seconds..."naw, I think we're carryin' about as much meat as we can."

"Whew!" Buck sighed. "If you'd decided to shoot it, I'd be waitin' for you back at the ranch!" he laughed.

Too Smart For His Hitches

"**D**amn! The pack horse is *gone!*"
I sat up in my sleeping bag that was covered in snow. "Holy shit, Buck—how will we carry everything out of here!?"

"Hey, Brady, any chance you could drive over a week early to hunt this year? The substitute, who was going to teach for me the first week in November can't cover that week."

"Sure, I should be able to do that. So, we'll be hunting on opening weekend?"

"Yeah, which could have some advantages for us. When hunters over in the Tyler Creek drainage area start shooting, it often drives the elk to higher ground where we'll be. If you could get to my place in Missoula about 3:00 on Thursday, October 21, I'll be home from teaching. We can pick up some groceries, then head for the ranch. This will give us a good chunk of Friday to organize our gear and get the horses ready. I'd like to take a pack horse with us when we ride into the Grouse Gulch area late Friday afternoon, and sleep on the ground so we'll be right where we want to be on Saturday morning. Think you'd be up for that?"

"Sure," I replied.

"Still thinking about taking a pack horse with us tomorrow, Buck?" I asked driving through the entrance gate to Buck's ranch at the Bearmouth, east of Missoula.

"Yes—in fact let me off by this first corral. I'll grab the horses we'll be ridin' and the young horse, who will be our pack horse, and meet you over at the ranch house. After you unpack your stuff, pull your car into the enclosure next to the garage and shut the gate so the horses don't chew on your paint over the next few days."

I pulled in front of the ranch house, raised the rear door to my Subaru Outback and carried my heavy suitcase up the front porch and into the foyer. My favorite room to stay in upstairs was Jamie's as it was on the south side of the house—farthest away from the trains that rumbled by on a regular basis just north of the ranch. After lugging my suitcase up the narrow staircase and into Jamie's room, I removed and organized my hunting gear, changed into my ranch clothes and headed back downstairs to move my car. Buck was right—the horses would gnaw the paint on your car if they could get to it. I asked Buck once why they do this, and he said he wasn't sure. "Some folks say it's to lick the salt from the roads that gets on your car; others say the horses do it when they're bored."

By the time I had parked my car, Buck was putting the three horses into the main corral across from the ranch house. "You'll be riding Ivan tomorrow, B and I'll be ridin' Jewell." Ivan, a sorrel with a white star on his forehead and white stockings, was by far the biggest of Buck's horse. The other horses respected Ivan and always deferred to him when it came to feed or attention. I was happy to hear I'd be riding him, as he was well-trained, obedient, sure footed, and was very familiar with the areas we'd be hunting.

"This is Joker," Buck said as he led the two year old into the corral off the tack room. "He'll be our pack horse tomorrow. I'm puttin' him in here for the night, so the other two horses don't pick on him all night."

The next morning after breakfast, I did up the dishes, split some logs and made kindling while Buck tended to the horses. He removed from the tack room, the pack frame Joker would be carrying later this afternoon.

After finishing my morning chores, I approached the corral and saw the pack frame lying on the ground. I'd never noticed it in the tack room before. It looked like an old, primitive wooden frame with lots of straps attached to it.

"Mind givin' me a hand with this, Brady?" Buck asked leading Joker over to the horizontal hitching post and securing his lead rope. "The frame's an old one, but it's in good shape. I got it from an old timer about five years ago for a great price; couldn't pass it up."

"Are there packs that fit on the frame, Buck?"

"Yes—heavy canvas packs that can hold quite a bit of stuff. We'll carry our sleeping bags in them when we head out this afternoon. If you wouldn't mind brushin' off his back before we put on his blanket, that would be great, Brady.

"Okay, now could you hold these straps up out of the way while I put the pack on his back?" Standing on the left side of the frame, he grabbed one end with his left hand, the other with his right and lifted it onto the extra thick saddle blanket. Buck adjusted the blanket while centering the frame. "Good...now just let the straps hang, and we'll figure out how to fasten them.... It's been a few years since I've used this pack.... These straps are obviously part of the cinches, so let's get them out of the way," he said threading them through the cinch rings and tightening them. "Now, let's bring the chest collar around... like this...and attach it with this strap.... There, that gets rid of that strap." He stepped back and eyed the straps that somehow fit around the horse's hind quarters. He then approached the horse and moved the straps to parts of the frame until they looked right. "Aaah, now I remember," he said attaching them, then adjusting them all to fit the young horse. He moved to each side of the horse, then to its front and back, as if taking a mental picture. "Okay, Brady, I think I've got it figured out. Now we can remove it; we'll put it back on before we leave later this afternoon. It shouldn't take me as long then. At least I know which is the front end now," he chuckled.

We spent the rest of the morning doing chores around the ranch and getting our gear ready to go.

After lunch, I made two deli sandwiches for each of us and put them into our daypacks. I included two Snickers bars and two apples each.

"When you come out to the corral would you bring the two dusters from the mud room, Brady? We'll be needin' them tonight."

"Ahhh, what are 'dusters', Buck?"

"The long, heavy oil skin coats that are hangin' in the mud room. Think of 'Man From Snowy River'."

"Oh...got it...yes, will do."

When I carried the dusters to the corral, Buck had tied the two horses we'd be riding to the vertical hitching post and was feeding them some grain.

"When you have everything out here that you want to take, B, we'll put the pack frame on Joker again, then load up the canvas packs before saddling our horses."

"Sounds good; I just have a few more things to bring out from the house." I felt excited yet a bit nervous as I thought about sleeping on the ground tonight without any shelter. But, I knew from past hunting stories Buck had shared with me over the years, that he'd done this many times when hunting by himself.

We put the pack frame on the two year old gelding with no problems. After attaching the canvas packs, we stuffed them with our sleeping bags, dusters and extra gear we wanted to bring. Then, we tightened down everything with the security straps.

On previous hunts with Buck, we left the ranch about 6:30 am while it was still dark to get to the high country at daylight. So, to be riding up the draw in the afternoon daylight seemed odd to me. Also, today, instead of continuing up the trail past Medicine Hill as we typically did, Buck headed west on one of the logging roads that we normally crossed on our way up to Bobcat Pass.

"This way will be easier on the horses, and will get us to where we want to be shortly before dusk," Buck said. Because I'd never ridden this way with Buck, he'd stop occasionally to point out various landmarks. "There's the beacon on top of Tyler Point," he said pointing to the southwest, after rounding one bend. "Below us and to the west is Tyler Creek where we fished with the kids years ago."

Buck was watching the shadows on the east-facing slopes. He wanted to allow enough afternoon daylight to reach our destination above Grouse. Several times he urged Jewell into a trot. When he did so, Ivan followed suit. The cool air made my eyes water and I had to blink frequently to clear them.

As the late afternoon light began to fade, Buck turned off the road and headed into the forest on a well-used game trail. Once in the tall surrounding Ponderosa trees, it became evening quickly. After a brief ride, he reined in Jewell and dismounted. "It's fairly flat here...let's tie up the horses, take their saddles and bridles off and secure them for the night. Find a nearby limb to hang your rifle from—barrel down, so nothing gets into it. Then, grab your duster and lay it down on a flat place so your sleeping bag stays dry. I'll tie the horses to different trees so they don't pick on each other tonight."

The flattest area I could find was a short section of the game trail, which turned out to be the perfect width for my body. After hanging my rifle upside down from a nearby, sturdy tree limb, I shook out my duster and laid it on the trail. I pulled my sleeping bag out of its compression sack and positioned it on top. Before settling in, I headed off the trail a ways to pee. *No stars tonight*, I observed looking skyward. *That means overcast—I hope we don't get rained on.* I made sure my headlamp and bear spray were withing reach, removed my boots and laid them on their sides nearby, removed my pants and jacket and bunched them together for a pillow. "G'night, Buck," I said crawling into my bag and zipping it closed. "Any animal that walks down this trail tonight is in for a big surprise."

"Night, Brady. Sweet dreams."

I had no idea what time it was when I woke up, but it was very dark. I could feel something cold hitting my face. *What the...it's SNOW!* "Buck, it's snowing!" I said in a loud whisper. I could hear Buck's bag rustle, then a pause as he poked his face out of his bag.

"Damn! What do you want to do, Brady?"

"I don't think there's a lot we can do while it's still so dark," I replied. "We'll have to hold tight 'til daylight when we can see."

"I agree...see you in the morning," he said disappearing into his bag again.

Buck had no trouble falling back to sleep because I could hear him snoring even though enshrouded in his mummy bag about ten yards away from me. It wasn't long before I was asleep again as well.

I hate being aroused from a peaceful sleep by the nagging urge to pee. When I poked my head out of my warm bag, I broke through the blanket of snow that neatly covered me. I could feel snow flakes falling on my head and face. "Oh, my God!" I said aloud. I kicked the inside of my sleeping bag, which removed much of the snow from the outside of my bag; then sitting up, I brushed the rest away so I could unzip it and keep the snow out. I pressed the light button on my Timex...*6: 02 am.* It wasn't yet light but the sky off to the right was a dull dark grey. I knocked the snow off my boots and slid my stockinged feet into their cold interiors. *Thank God I laid my boots on their sides.* On the way back to my bag after peeing, I could see both our horses. Ivan turned his head toward me, as if he wanted to tell me something. I glanced at where Buck had tied the pack horse but couldn't see him. *He must be on the other side of the tree, he was tied to.* I removed my boots, laid them on their sides, this time under part of the duster, and wriggled back into my bag. Its coziness was very welcome.

Then I heard Buck's bag rustle. "What the...." he said poking his head out. "Brady, I can't believe it's still snowing!"

"I know," I replied enjoying the warmth of my bag.

I could tell Buck was concerned because he wasted no time brushing off his bag and getting out. "First things first," he said heading off to pee. After finishing, he walked over to where our two horses were, paused, then walked over to where he'd secured Joker. "*Damn!* The pack horse is *gone!* He must have somehow worked the knot loose and taken off." Buck shouted out Joker's name a few times, thinking he might return if he was still nearby.

I sat up in my bag. "Holy shit, Buck. How will we carry everything out of here?"

After several seconds of silence, Buck said, "We'll have to put the pack frame on one of our horses and carry our bags and a saddle out on it—which means...Brady...*you* will be walkin' out of here," he added chuckling.

"Oh, my gosh!" I exclaimed knowing we were quite a ways from the ranch.

"What time is it, B?"

"Almost ten after six," I replied. "Should we get dressed and head out of here?"

"Well, no big hurry now. It'll take us awhile to put the pack saddle on one of our horses, load up our sleeping bags and coats and figure out a way to attach a saddle. And, besides, the elk will be bedded down until it stops snowing. Might as well sleep a bit more and wait 'til it's light enough to see what we're doin'. Whose idea was this anyway, Brady!" he added, removing his boots to get back in his sleeping bag.

We both managed to sleep for another hour; then decided to get moving. *Can't wait to get my gloves on,* I thought lacing up my hunting boots, then blowing on my frigid fingers to warm them. I stood up and stiffly walked about trying to stretch out my knotted muscles.

"Yep, you can see where he headed off," Buck said looking at the ground by the tree where Joker had been tied. Buck called out for him a couple more times.

"Think he'll make it back to the ranch, Buck?"

"We'll find out in a few hours. It'll take him awhile to find his way down to the ranch, since he's never been back here.... Well, we might as well get started. Let's go ahead and put the heavy blanket on Ivan because he's definitely the stronger horse."

Unfamiliar with the feel of this "saddle," Ivan kept looking back at us as we adjusted the straps to fit him. "Okay, let's put our bags and dusters and your saddle blanket in the bags; then we'll figure out how to secure your saddle to the pack.... I think if we center it on top of the pack and use its cinch to secure it, it should stay on—we'll just be walkin' outta here. We'll take turns ridin' Jewell, Brady...want to ride or walk first?"

"I think I'd like to walk first; it'll help me warm up a bit."

"Not a bad idea; in fact, I think I'll walk for a ways as well."

"You'll have to lead, Buck; I have no idea where we are."

"Gee, I don't either," Buck chuckled. "Maybe we should just follow Joker's tracks."

It felt good to walk, even though I had to carry my rifle and day pack. After about fifteen minutes, I began to warm up. I stopped Ivan and walked around the pack. "So far so good; the saddle seems to be secure," I said.

"Good!" Buck responded. "Well, Joker's headin' in the right direction," Buck said following the two year old's tracks with Jewel in tow. "Every once in awhile, you can see where he's stepped on his lead rope. Check this out. See the rope mark pressed into the snow...."

By the time we reached a logging road just west of Bobcat Pass, the snowfall began to ease and we could actually see a patch of clear sky to the west. Buck decided he'd ride for awhile as walking any distance was very hard on his bum knee—an old football injury. "I'll lead Ivan, Brady. Just walk behind him and keep an eye on the pack."

Every now and then I would look down and see another rope impression in the snow. *Incredible! How can a young horse that's never been back here know which way to head for home in he dark—and in the snow?*

"Now things will get interesting," Buck said as we left the road and headed north down the steep slope that would eventually take us back to the ranch. "This route will shave off some time. Let me know if the pack begins to shift and I'll tighten up the cinches."

Every now and then, we could hear hunters' shots from the Tyler Creek area to the west of us.

"Hopefully, that'll scare the critters over this way, Brady. We'll come back here tomorrow morning unless it snows again."

While I was disappointed I'd have no chance to shoot my rifle today, I was glad it was just the first of our three days hunting together. *There might still be a chance to shoot an elk. Think positive.*

Several hundred yards down the slope, the pack began to list to the right. *If the pack slides off Ivan and rolls underneath him, we could have a real disaster on our hands.* I ran to Ivan as fast as I could. I tried to halt the pack's slide and push it back up but it was difficult to do on the move, and while carrying my rifle. "*Buck, stop!* I need your help! The pack's beginning to slide off Ivan." Buck halted Jewell, quickly dismounted and jogged back to help me reposition the pack. Once it was centered again on Ivan's back, Buck tighten-up the cinches.

"You know, as long as we're stopped, I think I could use one of those sandwiches you made. How about you?" Buck asked.

"Well, I hate to see you eat alone," I responded removing my daypack.

"Did I ever tell you about the time I shot a bull and rode it down the hill in the snow?" Buck asked after taking a bite of his sandwich.

"No!" I responded anxious to hear more.

"Do you remember Hopper, the guy who took the trip to Las Vegas with us, and came to your wedding with me?"

"Yes."

"Well, I was hunting with him in Genoa Gulch in back of Tully's ranch when I shot this raghorn. He ran for about 20 yards and went down on a steep hillside, which made it too difficult to field dress him there, and too slippery for our horses to carry the heavy meat sacks out from there. So, I grabbed a rope out of my saddle bag and told Hopper to lead our horses down the hill to where it flattened out a bit. I tied the rope around the bull's antlers and head and started pulling him down the hill. When he began to slide on his own, I knelt on his side and lifted his head off the snow so I could slide down the rest of the steep hillside on him. It worked great—that is, until we slid into a mound of snow that brought us to an abrupt stop. Well, turned out that the 'mound' was a slash pile, and underneath it was a hibernating black bear. The bear came bursting out of the pile as I was getting off the elk. I yelled down to Hopper to shoot it, but he said he couldn't see it."

"Oh, my God—you must have been terrified!"

"I was! *And* I didn't have my rifle! Thank God the bear decided to run off."

"That's incredible, Buck!" I said, trying to imagine the chaotic scene.

After Buck and I finishing our sandwiches, we treated our horses to the apple cores and descended the remainder of the steeper slope that would lead us down to "Medicine Hill" just south of Buck's ranch. When we came to the logging road we'd taken yesterday, we could see the pack horse's tracks and where he'd stepped on the lead rope yet again. "How in the hell can a young horse who's never been back there find its way back home in the dark and in the snow?" I asked Buck.

"I'm not sure, but between their keen senses of smell, hearing and sight, they can find home." Buck nodded in the direction we'd just come from. "There's been times when I've gotten turned around back in there, given my horse its head, and its taken me back to the ranch—even after dark. I'm not sure how they do it, but I'm sure glad they can."

It was nearly 11:00 am when we walked through the gate at the southeast end of the ranch, still following Joker's tracks. Several yards inside the gate, we could see that one set of his tracks veered east, then a bit farther, another set of his tracks crossed back over them heading directly north; then yet another set of his tracks led to the west, where we wanted to go.

"Look at this, Brady. He tried all three of the different trails that lead down to the corral. Two of the trails are gated off; looks like he finally discovered the one with the open gate."

"That's incredible!"

When we emerged from the woods and walked toward the corral, guess who was standing there waiting for us, dangling lead rope and all! He looked at us and nickered as if to say, *"What took you guys so long?"*

"Let's see if you can untie *this* knot," Buck challenged the young horse tying his lead rope tightly to the horizontal hitching post.

"If he's smart enough to untie a lead rope, you'd better sell him, Buck. He's too smart for his 'hitches.'"

Buck laughed. "You got that right, Brady! I just may do that."

The Old Trapper's Cabin

I thought of the trapper, perhaps lying on this same side of the cabin—too sick to keep the stove going or to get water from the spring; too weak to head out and seek help—perhaps still snowed in. I wondered at what point he realized he might die here? *Maybe at some point, you just give in to the inevitable and become comatose?*

I'll never forget the first time I saw the old trapper's cabin back in Moyle Gulch south of Bearmouth, Montana. It was the first season I hunted with Buck Wiley after I retired from a career in public education. Buck had wanted to show me the old cabin back in Moyle the first day we hunted together that season, but we'd taken too much time following a cow moose and her calf.

"Okay, tomorrow, we're riding straight back to that old trapper's cabin I wanted to show you the first day," Buck said during breakfast. We'll take two fresh horses, so we can make good time riding back there. You'll be ridin' Sonny; I'll be riding Isaac. We'll head back up the same way we rode before, but instead of turning off the trail where we spotted the cow moose and her calf, we'll continue on the main trail."

"Sounds good, Buck; I'd love to see it!"

When we arrived at the curve where we'd veered right and run into the cow Moose and her calf, Buck motioned for us to continue south on the main trail. The trail continued up a slight grade for another quarter mile, then opened into a clearing. Unlike the lush, green grass we'd just ridden through into Moyle, the grass here was dry and sparse. To our right were two low-growing juniper bushes, that looked out-of-place given the lush surroundings we'd just ridden through. Buck directed Isaac to the right, leading us down into the clearing for about a hundred yards; then he turned left into the trees. He seemed to be following the blazes cut into some of the trees.

After a short distance riding through trees, I saw it. A small, very old, weather-worn log cabin nestled into a hallow below us—but...it had a blue plastic tarp covering its A-framed roof. A cylindrical, metal chimney protruded from the tarp. But, the cabin looked vacant. *That's strange!*

"There's the old trapper's cabin I've told you about, Brady," Buck announced as we approached its east side. The old logs looked a bit dilapidated, but they still formed a mostly vertical, protective wall.

Buck rode up to a tree on this side of the cabin and said, "Let's tie up the horses here and have a look around." Stacks of cut wood were piled on both sides of the small, low door; a heavy chopping block had been propped against the door—evidently to keep unwanted visitors from entering.

"Who's using this cabin, Buck?"

"A party that's been coming here for years during hunting season. Over the years, they've actually done some nice things inside. Let me show you." Buck rolled the chopping block out of the way and opened the door. "Watch your head as you go in." The light through the small open door was limited, as the cabin had no windows, but it allowed us to see the basic layout inside. Immediately to the left of the door was a small wood burning stove with a wide flat top—*probably for cooking*, I surmised. Just to the right of the door was a crude table with a couple small stumps on each side—*probably seats*. A tray of old silverware, a stack of plastic plates, cups, glasses and other kitchen utensils sat on a primitive counter top on the left side of the cabin. Above it, several different-sized pots and pans, and a lantern hung from nails secured to one of the lodge pole beams.

"What's that for?" I asked pointing to a keg spigot on the end of a pipe.

"For water. There's an underground spring outside this wall just a few feet away from the cabin. They plumb into it when they're here, so they don't have to bring water inside with buckets. Pretty clever, huh!"

"Oh, my gosh—'tap water'!" I chuckled. Bunk beds constructed from lodgepole and pieces of plywood were secured to the north wall; the same to the east wall.

"This is incredible!" I exclaimed. "What a neat hunting cabin! This is the *real thing*!"

"I know; if they ever stop coming here, I will definitely be taking this spot over...." Buck bent down and peered under the kitchen counter. "Hey, want a beer?"

I bent down and looked. "Shit, it's a whole case of Miller Lite! Ahaa...I'd better not, Buck; they probably wouldn't appreciate it."

"Go ahead, B—help yourself. They'd want you to, and you can enjoy it with your lunch. This is as good a place as any to eat our lunches."

"Okay," I replied removing one of the cans and opening it. "Wow! Now, *that's* a cold beer!" I said smacking my lips. I knew better than to ask Buck if wanted a sip because he doesn't drink. "Is there any history about the trapper, who lived in this cabin, Buck?"

"I understand there's a little—but not much was recorded. The relatives of a family that homesteaded in the Bearmouth area, the Websters, said that the trapper, who lived back here would come out of the woods a couple of times during the year to sell his furs and get supplies. One year when he didn't show, some guys got concerned, traveled in here and found him near death. He'd evidently injured a leg, fallen ill from infection, and was too weak to get out for help. He died not long after they took him out."

"Man, I can't imagine living in this small primitive cabin all year—especially during the long, cold winters! He must have been one tough guy...and, able to live by himself."

"Yeah, can you imagine how much wood you'd have to cut during the summer to get through the winter without freezing to death! And how challenging it must have been to find enough food to survive! I can understand why he built the cabin here next to the spring...but finding enough food must have been a constant challenge. And then when he finally got a deer or an elk—or a moose, he'd have to haul the meat back here—by *himself*!"

I finished the last of my sandwich and the beer, and put the empty can back into its slot in the case under the countertop. "Can you imagine the conversation this empty can will initiate!?"

"Yeah, let's make tracks," Buck chuckled. "Time to pretend we're the trapper in search of meat!"

We closed the door, rolled the chopping block up against the door, saddled up and headed out of the hallow. Near the top of the rise, I looked back for one last glimpse. *What a fantastic elk camp,* I thought.

For the next two years, we continued to use the elk camp that Buck and his sons erected before each hunting season in Grouse Gulch. The main shelter was basically a large canvas tent framed in by slender lodgepole pine sections that supported a blue tarp, which not only covered the tent itself but extended a few feet beyond the tent. The front extension protected firewood stacked on both sides of the tent's entrance. To the left of the tent were two established trees with a hefty wooden beam between them for hanging game. About 20 yards in back of the tent to its right was a small corral.

Four stairs led up to the floor of the tent, which according to Buck was supported by a foundation of lodge poles laid out close together horizontally and covered by green outdoor carpeting. The entrance consisted of two flaps that could be tied back or zipped shut.

A small wood burning stove was to the right inside the tent, its chimney rising up through a hole in the canvas protected by sheet metal flashing; then through an opening in the plastic to the outside. One crude bunk was to the left of the entrance; the other against the rear wall. The bunks consisted of pieces of plywood lying on top of framed lodge poles secured to the wood floor. An orange, cylindrical cooler served as the refrigerator.

During the first of those last two seasons at Grouse, I had the opportunity to visit the trapper's cabin again—only this season, no plastic tarp covered its roof.

"Buck, there's no one using it this year!"

"Yeah...interesting. If they don't use it again next year, I just might take it over. Let's have a look around."

We dismounted and tied up the horses. The chopping block was off to the side and the door was halfway open. The door's top hinge had given way; its bottom was resting on the ground. The small wood burning stove was in tact but part of its chimney lay on the cabin floor. One end of the kitchen shelving was also on the earthen floor, and the small table to the right of the door was broken. A few of the lodge poles that supported the tarp during hunting season were broken and hanging downward into the interior.

"Looks to me like a bear got in here and busted up a few things while it was rummaging around," Buck surmised.

I took a few pictures while Buck surveyed the damage and made mental notes; then we remounted to resume our day's hunt.

During the second of those last two seasons in the Grouse camp, an unexpected visit by a Dept. of Natural Resource employee marked its doom. Buck and I had returned from a long morning hunt empty-handed and tired. We had just finished our lunches seated outside in the unusually warm November sunshine in just our flannel shirts. I stood up from the chopping block I was seated on and groaned as I stretched out my back.

"How's your back these days?" Buck asked before taking a big bite from his Gala apple.

"Well, If I could just get rid of this damned sciatic nerve pain down my left leg, I'd be fine. I keep hopin' that ridin' a horse and huntin' will pop things back into place."

"Have you seen a doc about it yet?"

"No, but if it doesn't improve soon, I think I'll have to."

I'd injured my back three years prior while helping a friend carry a heavy oak desk up a flight of stairs to his second story. I was bent over walking up the stairs backwards when I felt something tear in my back. Instead of setting the desk down, I bit my lip and completed the next several steps to the top. I knew when I set the desk down and stood up that I'd done something bad to my back.

Buck stood up, stretched out his back, took one last bite from his apple and headed over to his horse to share the core. "Well...I know this will come as a surprise, B, but it's my nap time."

As usual, Buck was sawing logs within minutes of lying down on top of his sleeping bag. *How does he do that?* I wondered staring at the tent's ceiling and listening to needles from the surrounding trees occasionally hit the overhanging tarp. Then, at some point as I drowsed, I thought I heard a voice. I held my breath and listened intently. It sounded like two guys talking off in the distance. *Couldn't be,* I thought. *This is so far back...no one comes back here.* Then, I heard the voices again, much closer this time. *No doubt about it, we have company.*

"Buck!"

"Ugh?"

"I hear voices and they're getting closer."

"What!?" Buck blurted sitting up and listening. As soon, as he heard them, he stood up and unzipped the tent flaps.

"Howdy," hailed one of the two visitors. They were both dressed more like hikers than hunters.

"Howdy," Buck replied. "What's goin' on?"

"Well, my name's Guthrie from the Dept. of Natural Resources; this is my assistant. We're back here to investigate a complaint we received from a Buck Wiley re: the condition of the creek back here due to free ranging cattle."

"Well, I'm the guy who wrote the letter," Buck replied. "You no doubt noticed some of the damage on your way in here, but I'll be happy to show you around."

"No, that's alright, we'll take a look around." He looked downstream, then back at Buck. "Is this your hunting camp?"

"Yep."

"Are you aware that you can't have a permanent structure back here?"

"Yes, but I know that I can set up a hunting camp for up to fourteen days. We always take down the tent after we hunt."

"That's correct, but...it looks like you have a permanent lodgepole structure around it, *and* a corral."

"Well, we've been hunting back here from this same camp for over ten years and we've never had anyone express a concern or complaint about it."

I could tell Buck was beginning to get agitated.

"Are you guys back here because of my letter about McGrady's cattle, or are you back here about this hunting camp?"

Buck's directness got to the guy, who paused before responding. He was no doubt thinking, *these two guys have rifles; we're not armed.*

He replied very diplomatically, "We're here to follow up on your letter...but I just want to make sure you're aware of the State regulation regarding permanent structures."

"I'm well aware of the State regulation," Buck replied coldly looking hard at the man. His companion remained silent the entire time.

"Well...have a good hunt...we're going to walk down the creek a ways and check things out."

Buck didn't respond and stood on the top step while the two men headed east and disappeared.

"What was *that* all about?" I asked.

"Well, I wrote a complaint letter to the Dept. of Natural Resources about McGrady, a rancher who's been letting his cattle run wild back here. His cows are destroying the integrity of the stream and trampling this entire creek drainage area. But this DNR asshole seems more concerned about this hunting camp being here, than he does about the damage McGrady's cattle are doing to these parts."

"Well, I hope the DNR makes McGrady stop grazing his cattle back here," I said stuffing my sleeping bag into its sack.

I could tell Buck was upset by the attitude of the DNR guy as we rode back to the ranch that afternoon. He wasn't his normal peppy, joking self, and no deer or elk came into view to help him forget about this encounter.

I was out mowing the lawn the following spring, when Patsy brought the phone to me. "It's Buck," she said.

"Brady, thought I'd give you a jingle and see how your back's doin' these days."

"Well...about the same, unfortunately. I've still got this damned sciatica. A few weeks back, I told my doctor that I wanted to get an MRI to find out what's causing it because three years of puttin' up with this constant pain is enough. He agreed, so I have an appointment for an MRI next week. I'll let you know what the results are.

"Hey, have you ridden back to the camp yet?"

"Ya mean the elk camp that *used* to be there?"

"What do you mean, 'used to be there'?"

"The camp is no longer there, Brady. Do you remember the guys who paid us a visit at the elk camp last hunting season?"

"Yeah."

"Well, they must've come back in there sometime this spring and leveled the entire camp with a chainsaw."

"What!! Why would they do that?"

"Remember the guy who did most of the talking, Guthrie?"

"Yeah, the DNR guy?"

"Yep. Well, I found out he's pretty tight with McGrady, the cattle rancher I complained about. I guess it was the rancher's way of getting back at me for initiating the complaint against him. It's interesting that no one from DNR or Fish and Game ever expressed any concern about that elk camp or did anything to it until now—*after* I registered the complaint about the rancher."

"Are you going to file a complaint with the Dept. of Natural Resources?"

"Naw...technically, you're not supposed to have any permanent structure set up on forest lands."

"But, it really wasn't a permanent structure was it? You took the tent down after hunting season."

"Well, we removed the tent and stove and all the gear, but not the lodge pole framing and the horse corral, which I'm sure they would argue is 'permanent.' Fortunately, they didn't find the storage bin back in the woods, where I have all the kitchen stuff.

"Anyway, Brady, I was wonderin' if you could drive over this summer and help me salvage a few things for the new elk camp?"

"Sure...I could come out in June right after you're done with the school year."

"That would be perfect. I can have John help me with stuff you and I don't get done."

"Where's the new elk camp going to be?"

"You remember the old trapper's cabin in Moyle Gulch that I showed you?"

"Yes."

"Well, the party that had been using it for years, hasn't used it for two years in a row now. So, I guess a *new party* is taking it over."

"Oh my gosh...that's incredible, Buck! That cabin is so neat—it's the real deal! But, won't the DNR come in and tear *it* down?"

"No, because it's an historic building. They can't tear it down."

"*Perfect!* Well...how about I come over the third week in June. Your school year will be over and Patsy will be finishing up her school year that week, so it would be a good time for me to be out of here."

"That would be great, Brady. I'll keep in touch."

"So sorry to hear about the Grouse elk camp, Buck," I said after arriving at the ranch in June. "You said it was pretty much demolished, huh?"

"Wait 'til you see it, Brady. They really did a number on it."

The next morning, worried a bit about how my back would hold up riding back to Grouse and Moyle, I did the back stretches my doctor had given me, before breakfast on the living room carpet.

Buck walked into the living room from the kitchen to join me. He began to stretch out his bad knee. "Look at us—a couple of ol' farts!" We both enjoyed a good chuckle.

"How's your back this morning, B?"

"It's a bit stiff—probably from all the driving the past couple of days."

After breakfast, while Buck fed our horses and a young pack horse some grain at the hitching posts, I made sandwiches in the kitchen, tossing in two apples and some Snickers bars before heading out to the corral. After helping Buck load items into the pack, I brushed off our horses' backs and bellies, then began to pick their hooves. Each time I bent over and cradled the horses' legs, my lower back tightened up, so I had to stand up straight and stretch after releasing each leg.

After fitting our pack horse with the pack, we secured the bags on the frame, loaded them with the items we wanted to take, then cinched them up. When I swung the heavy saddle I'd be using onto Sonny, I felt a painful twinge, so stood up straight and stretched out my back.

"You okay?" Buck asked.

"Yeah...just a bit stiff. I think once I start ridin' I'll be fine."

My back actually did feel pretty good as we rode up the gulch toward the south boundary of Buck's property. "What a beautiful morning!" I exclaimed as we emerged from the brushy fir trees onto the first logging road south of Buck's fence line. We looked out over the valley below us to the north as we rested our horses. What a contrast this morning was to hunting season, when we'd ride up this way in the dark and return in the dim gray of a late November afternoon.

I tried to visualize what the elk camp would look like as we headed off the Bobcat Pass logging road down toward Grouse Gulch. As we approached the small wooden bridge, I looked over at the area that was once the elk camp. It was *vacant*.

"Oh my God!" I gasped. The lodge poles that provided the foundation and framing for the canvas tent and the blue tarp that covered the tent had been cut into short pieces and were stacked in a pile. And all the poles that once formed the horse corral were cut up and lay stacked in a separate pile. "Why would they destroy the corral too, Buck? People who ride back into here could have at least used it to rest their horses."

"I know—they really did a number on this place. *Assholes!* Fortunately they didn't find our storage box. Let's tie up the horses and I'll show you where it is." Buck led me into some thick timber and brush just south of where the tent once stood. I could understand why the DNR guys had missed it. Well shrouded by low-growing firs was a metal box framed in by sections of hefty lodge poles. Buck showed me the bite marks on the tin where a bear had tried to tear through it a few years ago. In places, the bear had bitten clear through the metal.

"Gives you an idea of what they could do to a person, huh!" Buck emphasized.

"I'll say...wow!"

"I'm just going to leave this box and its contents here for now; John and I can come in before hunting season, disassemble it and reassemble it at the new camp. Let's go salvage the pieces of plywood for the bunks."

We returned to the larger pile of cut up lodge poles, close to where the tent frame once stood, and tossed aside pieces until we spotted the rectangular pieces of plywood. Once we'd found them all, Buck drilled holes along one edge of each one, so we could tie two pieces together with orange baling twine. This allowed our horses to carry two pieces of plywood on their backs. *Kind of like sandwich boards,* I thought as I helped Buck position and tie the pieces together.

"We'll have to make sure these boards don't get hung up on anything as we lead the horses back into Moyle, B. We'll just take it nice and slow. Man, it's going to be a warm one today," Buck said wiping his face with his kerchief.

I felt sorry for the horses as they schlepped the heavy, awkward pieces of plywood up the grade from Grouse; then through some of the narrow passages into Moyle. Several times along the way, we had to halt the horses, back them up, and adjust our heading before moving forward again. Periodically, Buck would get the chain saw out of the pack, fire it up and cut through a tree or large limb that had fallen over the Moyle trail during the winter. Nearly two hours later, we arrived at the trapper's cabin.

"Let's get this plywood off of them and see if they'll drink from the spring on the other side of the cabin," Buck directed.

After the horses had their fill, we tied them to nearby trees with their lead ropes, removed their bridles and loosened their cinches, for we'd be here awhile.

"Well, let's take a look inside and see what we've got here," Buck suggested, lifting the bottom of the door off the ground so he could open it farther. "This door's obviously going to need some repair," he noted. "The wood stove and metal work are going to need some attention too, but that's okay, I've got that stuff from the other stove. The supports for the bunks look to be okay—just need to be adjusted a bit. And, we can redo this table," Buck added moving pieces of the broken table to the center of the cabin. "In fact, let's do that first so we have a place to eat our lunch. If you'll grab the drill and screws out of the pack, I'll get these pieces organized."

Buck laid the table's top onto the dirt floor and centered a cut log on top of it. "Okay help me turn this table over and we'll drive a few of these long screws through the top into the end of this log."

After we secured the table top, we cleared out the spot to the right of the door so the table would sit somewhat level on the dirt floor; then rolled the individual cut logs that served as seats into place on either side of the table. "There...how about lunch, B?"

"Sounds good, I'll bring in our daypacks *and* our water bottles. Man, it's got to be in the high 80s today!"

As we ate our sandwiches, Buck explained how he planned to repair various areas of the cabin. "After lunch, we'll make sure these bunk frames are secure and level, then screw the slats of plywood to them. Later this summer, John and I will replace some of the broken lodge poles for the roof, fix the shelving for the kitchen, get the stove all set up and build a new cache box for our camp utensils. That way, all we'll need to do before hunting season is pull the plastic tarp over the roof, secure the ends, then stock this place with our camp supplies. After we finish lunch, I'll cut down some trees and buck 'em up for firewood if you'll stack the bolts on each side of the doorway, B."

"Sounds good," I replied finishing the last bite of my sandwich.

I stood up and stretched out my back and rubbed my left buttock attempting to ease the sciatic pain.

"How's it feelin'?"

"It's a little tight; think I'll step out and do my back stretches before hauling some wood."

"Tell ya what, B...let's get these bunks squared away first, then you can lie down for awhile while I cut down some trees. That's pretty much a one man job until I start buckin' them up."

"Okay, sounds good to me," I responded ducking as I walked out the low doorway to stretch.

We spent the next 35 minutes adjusting the lodgepole bed frames so they were pretty much level; then secured the plywood to them with wood screws.

"Close enough!" Buck exclaimed. "Now, test 'em out and rest your back while I cut down a few trees."

I rolled up the flannel shirt I'd brought along, to use as a pillow, and lay on my back looking up at the blue sky through the open lodgepole rafters. I listened to the horses as they used their rear hooves to dislodge the pesky horse flies. Every now and then the horses would shake their bodies to shoo away the flies, rattling their tack in the process. I could hear Buck getting the chain saw ready, then pulling twice before it roared to life. The harsh rattle of the idling saw grew fainter as Buck walked a ways up the slight slope to the north of the cabin. Then, the saw revved and bit into a tree. Within seconds, the slender lodge pole crashed to the ground with a loud thud. More idling, then after another outburst of the noisy saw, a second tree crashed down.

A louder, odd-sounding crash accompanied the third tree as it descended. *"What the...!?"* I heard Buck exclaim.

I got up and looked north to where Buck was now walking back toward the cabin slightly to the east. "What was that, Buck?"

"I'm not sure...but something was in that grove of trees...Oh my God...it's all their camp gear!" Buck declared turning off the chainsaw.

As I entered the grove of trees, I spotted a blue plastic garbage can with one of its handles severed; the other handle sported a piece of broken rope. The can, now missing its lid due to the fall, had obviously been hanging in this group of trees, and had been freed by the tree Buck had just felled. I righted the can and we began to look inside. "Wow...two lanterns."

"Looks like the glass in one broke during the fall," Buck noted. "And, here's all their silverware...plates...cups...."

"Do you think they'll come back for any of this stuff, Buck?"

"I don't think so; they haven't been back now for at least two years...so, guess it's *ours* now! Let's put the lid back on and carry it into the cabin. We'll secure the lid so no critters will get into it; then John and I will go through it when we come back later this summer. We can use some of this stuff to supplement our camp utensils."

After carrying the plastic storage bin into the cabin, Buck headed back outside toward his chain saw. "I'll cut-up what I've taken down so far and you can begin carrying the bolts back to the cabin, B. Just stack them up on either side of the door; John or Jeff and I will split them later."

The bolts weren't very heavy, maybe 20 pounds each, so my back didn't bother me at first. Then, as it tightened up, I began using my foot to roll the bolts down toward the front of the cabin. *Hopefully this will help; sure don't want my back to seize-up back here.* However, by the time I'd stacked the bolts from the first two trees, I had to lie on the ground and do my back stretches again. The muscles in my lower back felt taut and the sciatic pain down my left leg was constant and intense.

Spotting me lying on the ground, Buck shouted, "You okay?"

"Just doin' a few stretches, Buck. My damned back's tightening up again. I think it will be okay in a few minutes."

When my back felt a bit less tight, I stood up and began to transport bolts from the third fallen tree, but almost immediately, my back tightened up. *I'd better stop or I may not be able to ride outta here!*

I alerted Buck.

"Okay, just rest your back, Brady. I'll finish up this tree; then we'll head out. Do you have any pain medication?"

"Not here, but I do have some back at the ranch."

As I lay on one of the bunks in the cabin hoping my lower back muscles would relax, I thought of the trapper, perhaps lying on this same side of the cabin—too sick to keep the stove going or to get water from the spring; too weak to head out and seek help—perhaps still snowed in. I wondered at what point he realized he might die here? *Maybe at some point, you just give in to the inevitable and become comatose?*

I could hear Buck reloading the bags and securing them; then cinching down our saddles. I felt fortunate to have someone like Buck here to help me at a time I was so incapacitated.

"Okay, B. Make sure you have everything you carried in, and let's head for the ranch. I'll lead Sonny over to those bolts and you can use one of them to get in the saddle."

I attempted to sit up from the bunk but the muscles in my lower back prevented me from doing so. I rolled onto my right side and, using my arms, was able to push myself up, then stand. The first step I took sent a sciatic shock down my left leg, and I hobbled out of the cabin, bent over, to my horse. I raised my right foot up onto the bolt, stood on it, put my left foot into the stirrup, and grabbing the reins and withers in my left hand, hoisted myself into the saddle. I grimaced as I awkwardly drug my right leg over the cantle. Sitting in the saddle brought some temporary relief, but as soon as Sonny began walking, I felt the sciatic pain shoot down my left leg. *Oh, my God, how in the hell am I going to make it all the way back to the ranch if I'm already in this much pain!?*

"How ya doing, B?"

"Ah, not too good, Buck. Hopefully things will improve after we ride for a bit." I could tell by the look on Buck's face he was concerned.

"Ya know what...instead of riding back the way we came in, I think we'll take the logging roads down to Tyler Creek and ride back to the ranch that way. I think there will be less jarring on your back going this route."

"Sounds good to me, Buck; appreciate it. Sorry I'm being such a wimp."

"Hey, no problem. You know what they say, B...better you than me."

Unfortunately, the sciatic pain didn't subside as we rode. I winced each time Sonny stepped—particularly when heading downhill. It was a long, painful, conversation-less ride down the logging roads leading to Tyler Creek.

What a relief when we neared the bottom of our long descent from Moyle, and I could hear the flow of the creek! Even though we were still a few miles from the ranch, I knew the roughest part of the ride was over, which encouraged me to keep going.

The trail along Tyler periodically crossed the creek. I loved the hollow sound the horses' hooves made when walking on the rocks below the moving stream. I recalled the times Buck and I had fished along this creek and even camped here in a tent before the ranch house had been finished. *There's the tree with the cougar claw marks on it*, I remembered riding past the big Ponderosa pine right next to the trail. Buck had pointed the marks out to me on one of our rides on this trail years ago, well before we had kids.

After riding along the creek for about 45 minutes, I recognized the crossing where a tree limb knocked John from the horse he and Ashley, our youngest daughter, were riding one summer when we were visiting the Wileys. Ashley, who was sitting in the saddle saw it coming and ducked below the limb; John was caught by surprise and the limb knocked him off the horse into the creek—fortunately with no serious injury.

After crossing to the east side of Tyler, I recognized the open area where we had fished with our kids one summer. The trout were small but the smiles wide when the kids caught one.

Not too much farther now. Just walk the horses around the cattle guard, ride through this lower field....

Okay, now to the top of the hill; then down to the ranch, I thought as we approached the last hill before reaching the ranch. I glanced down at the alfalfa field where Buck and I plucked gophers with our .22's during the summers when I'd drive over to visit him.

"Just about there, B...hang on," Buck encouraged as we rode down the rough dirt road above the large pond to our left.

Our horses began to whinny as they neared the ranch, and the horses out in the fields responded welcoming us back.

When we reached the hitching posts, Buck cupped his hands to support my left foot; then provided some resistance while I slowly lowered myself to the ground. I couldn't stand up straight.

"I'll take care of the horses, Brady while you go in and shower. Take one of your pain pills and just relax; I'll be in in a bit."

"Thanks, Buck—my back really appreciates it," I said hobbling hunched over toward the house.

I fixed myself a sandwich so I'd have some food in my stomach then took a pain pill. It began to take effect as the soothing hot shower washed the sweat and dirt from my aching body. After toweling off and slipping into some clean clothes, I slowly lowered myself into the cushioned rocking chair in the living room and shut my eyes, grateful to no longer be on the horse.

"How's the back, B?" Buck asked as he entered the front door.

"Well, this chair sure beats the saddle right now. I think the pain pill and the hot shower are definitely helping. Hopefully by tomorrow morning my back will be relaxed enough for me to head for home."

"Think you'll be seeing your neurosurgeon when you get back?"

"I'll *definitely* be seeing my neurosurgeon when I get back! And, I'm going to tell him I want to schedule a surgery to repair the herniated disc; I want to be ready for hunting this fall."

"Good move, B. After I clean up, I'll fix us some grub then you can hit the sack early."

When I awoke at 6:30 the next morning, I could hear Buck rummaging around down in the kitchen. I lay on my left side trying to determine if my lower back muscles had relaxed a bit during the night. Using my left arm, I pushed myself up until I was sitting up in the bed. *So far so good*, I thought contemplating my next move. I moved my legs to the side of the bed without much pain, but as soon as I lowered my left leg to the floor, I felt the sciatic shock in my buttock and down my left leg. *Shit! It's going to be a looooong drive back home.*

"Oh, oh," Buck said as he heard me slowly and unrhythmically descend the stairs. "Doesn't sound good, B...."

"I was hoping a good night's sleep would improve things, Buck, but I've still got this damned sciatica. It's going to be a long drive back home."

"Ahh, sorry to hear that B. Fix yourself some coffee; I'll get some eggs and sausage goin' here shortly."

"Thanks, Buck. I'm sorry for being such a pain in the...*back*," I chuckled.

"Hey, no problem, B. I'm just glad it's not me; I've got irrigation pipes to move today."

After breakfast, I took another pain pill then headed upstairs to pack up my stuff, trying to not think about the long drive back to Spokane. *I'll definitely stay at my brother's place tonight; trying to drive all the way to Lynden would be insanity.*

"Let me know when your bag is ready, Brady, and I'll carry it down for you; then we'll load up your cooler with some elk meat."

"That would be great, Buck—thank you!"

Man, I sure hope my Doc has a surgery opening soon, I thought as I packed my suitcase. *Hope there's no complications...I wonder how long it'll take me to recover? What if my surgeon says no horseback riding? No hunting? No skiing?*

"Okay, Buck, my suitcase is ready," I announced after slowly reaching the foyer below the stairs.

"Let's drive your car back to the garage so it will be closer to the freezer," Buck suggested after sliding my suitcase into the back of the Subaru. When we reached the garage, he removed the blue and white cooler and took it into the garage.

"You're too generous," I said as I watched him fill my cooler with packages of elk meat.

"No problem. I sure appreciate you drivin' over to help me with the new elk camp, B. I put in some burger, breakfast sausage, a few roasts and a couple rolls of thuringer," Buck said sliding the cooler into the back of the Subaru next to my suitcase. "Hey, at least it's a beautiful day for a drive!" he added.

"Thanks so much, Buck. I'd stay and help you move irrigation pipe, but...probably wouldn't be too much help today," I chuckled. "I'll give you a call when I get back home, and let you know when my surgery will be."

Buck gave me a much gentler hug than usual. "Do that, and thanks again for driving over, Brady. Have a safe trip back."

I tooted the traditional *"Shave and a Haircut"* beat as I headed down the long driveway.

The surgery to repair my herniated disc that summer was very successful and I was back hunting with Buck in the fall. The first day of this hunting season, we didn't see a deer or an elk, but Buck didn't seem particularly concerned. I think he was more excited for me to see the new trapper's cabin.

The first difference I noticed as we approached the cabin was the blue tarp snugly covering the roof, and the stove pipe protruding from its southwest corner. The second thing I noticed was a hitching post on the east side of the cabin, and the recently built corral about 25 yards in front of the cabin. "Wow, nice job on the corral, Buck!"

"Thank you, B! If you'll grab the eggs and hash browns out of your saddle bag, I'll show you the inside," he added removing the heavy chopping block from in front of the door. "Notice that you don't have to lift the door off the ground now to open it—and, it even *latches!*"

"I'm impressed, Buck, and looks like you have a good supply of wood," I added looking at the stacks on both sides of the door under the overhang of the tarp.

"Yeah, my daughter's husband, Justin came back here a few weeks ago, split all this and stacked it."

The open door let just enough light into the cabin so that I could see the dark outlines of the interior. But, it wasn't until Buck lit the propane lantern hanging on a nail from one of the cross poles, that its yellow glow revealed the organizational improvements he'd made. The small wood-burning stove with its wide metal top was inside the door to the left and ready to go. A stack of kindling lay to its left; some smaller split wood and a water bucket to its right. Pots and pans hung neatly above the kitchen counter along the west wall. The orange Gatorade cooler from the old camp stood to the right of the kitchen counter. The sleeping bags in their stuff sacks hung from nails over the bunks to the right.

"Man, what a great job you guys did on this cabin, Buck! You've made so many improvements since June!"

"Thanks. It's taken some time and effort, but it's also been fun getting it ready to go—just for *you*, B."

"Aww, I appreciate it, Buck." I quickly glanced under the kitchen counter, "but...where's the Miller Lite?"

Buck laughed. "Haven't gotten to that yet, B. Next trip.... Well, let's get a fire goin'. No flares this year—my railroad connection retired, but this tube stuff works pretty well. Want to try it?"

"Sure," I replied wadding up some paper and placing it in the stove. I added some kindling, a few strategic squeezes of the gelled fire starter, a couple small logs, then struck a match.

"Won't take the stove long to heat this place up; here's some nails to hang your clothes on when you get too warm," Buck said pointing to several nails partially driven into a cross pole over the bunks. He poured some water from one of the buckets into a couple sauce pans. "I'll get some water boilin' on the stove top so we can wash up and have water for dishes."

I could tell Buck was very pleased with how organized the kitchen was: pots and pans hanging from their nails, silverware and knives in a container; plastic dishwashing tub, soaps, towels, washcloths together at the north end of the kitchen counter. "While the water's heating up, we can lay out our mattress pads and sleeping bags. Just add some air if you want more support, B."

We both had removed our jackets by the time the water began to boil, and after a five minute rolling boil, Buck moved the sauce pans off to the sides of the wide stovetop. "And now, Brady the big decision—chili or ravioli?"

I laughed. "Ahhh, let's see...ravioli."

"Damn! I was hopin' you'd say chili!" he said chuckling.

He opened two cans of ravioli, removed another sauce pan from one of the nails twirling it by its handle and placed it on the stove top. "Would you like some bread with that, B?"

"Please."

"Toasted?"

"But of course," I smiled, enjoying the proud roll Buck was on.

While the ravioli was warming in the pan, Buck placed two pieces of bread on the stove top, and flipped them over with a spatula when the down side had browned.

He divided the hot ravioli onto two plates. "Toast!" he announced placing a browned slice on my plate with the spatula.

"Such fine cuisine, Buck!"

"Nothing but the best, B," he laughed.

"What time do you want to get up tomorrow?" I asked after a few bites.

"Well, probably about 6:00. By the time we finish breakfast, button up this place and get the horses ready, that should be about right. No sense staying back here another night—there's obviously no elk in this area."

After we finished eating, we wiped the plates and silverware off with a paper towel, which we tossed into the fire, then washed and rinsed the plates and utensils in the dishwashing tub.

"You're so organized, Buck!"

"Thank you, B."

Dusk comes early back in Moyle Gulch and darkness isn't far behind. After we refilled the horses' buckets with water for the night, we made sure the corral gate was secure; then brushed our teeth, peed, put a couple more logs on the fire, turned off the lantern, then slid into our sleeping bags. I reached out to make sure I could reach my headlamp and bear spray on the stump near my bunk...just in case. Buck's friend, Bill Werner, who tracks mountain lions and bears for Montana Fish, Wildlife and Parks, told Buck that there were a couple of grizzly bears back in this area. *Hopefully, they're hibernating by now,* I thought to myself.

"Thanks for setting up this camp, Buck; it's incredible that we're actually staying inside the same cabin a trapper used over 100 years ago."

"You're welcome, B. You helped set up part of it as well! Yeah, every time I come back here, I think of how tough that guy must've been to live back here by himself, year round. When he wasn't trapping, he'd be cutting wood, hunting, hauling meat back here to dry, and, in the winter, stoking the stove to keep from freezing to death. I can't imagine…. You know what they say, Brady—better him than us! Well, goodnight, B; don't let the bears bite."

"G'night, Buck." As usual, Buck was snoring within just a few minutes, which made my getting to sleep a challenge. While waiting for sleep to overtake me, I recalled how crippled up my back was the last time I was back here, and the long painful ride out. It made me think of the injured trapper, who unlike me, wasn't able to get out for help. I thought about the first time I'd seen this cabin, and how envious I was of the hunting party using it. And now we were actually staying in it! I felt so fortunate! *Thank you, Lord!*

The next thing I heard and saw was Buck wadding up some paper to get the fire going again. He held his little flashlight in his mouth as he did so.

"Brrrzy! Get's a little chilly when that fire goes out," Buck declared tossing in some newspaper, kindling and some small logs before striking a match. He then returned to his sleeping bag. "Think I'll let the stove warm things up a bit before we get serious about anything else. What time is it, Brady?"

I pressed the light button on my watch. "Five forty-five," I replied yawning. "Man, don't know why I'm still sleepy; I only slept for…nine hours." Buck let go with one of his infamous rancid farts. "Oh my God…I guess I'm awake now," I said coughing and burying my face in my sleeping bag.

"It's a good thing my farts don't stink," he replied laughing.

About ten minutes later when the wood stove had begun to overtake the chill in the room, we unzipped our sleeping bags, lit the lantern and got dressed. I tended the fire while Buck removed the feed sacks from the metal garbage can, shook more pellets into the horses' trays and carried them out to the corral.

Once the horses were fed and watered, we scrambled the eggs in one fry pan, and fried up the hash browns in another skillet.

"Where do you want to hunt this morning," I asked as we ate breakfast?

"We'll head out of here and see what's going on in Grouse. If we don't see any critters there, we'll head east a bit and make a big loop back to that bald hill behind Tulley's ranch."

After washing the pans and silverware, we deflated our mattress pads, stuffed our sleeping bags into their sacks, finished our morning routines, and gathered up our gear.

I carried the lantern while Buck led Isaac to the rear of the cabin where we saddled him, slipped the reins on him and walked him to the hitching post. We then did the same with Sonny. After making sure we had everything we wanted to take back, we slid our rifles into the scabbards, mounted up, and rode north toward the trail we'd ridden in on. The canyon was just beginning to lighten as we turned left onto the trail.

About 15 minutes into our ride, after we'd passed through the lush, grassy area, I saw Buck signal me to get off my horse. I stepped off into the hillside to our left, grabbed my rifle and walked up beside him.

"There's a buck up ahead," he whispered. "Walk slowly up the trail and you should be able to see him. He's on the left side of the trail in the trees," he pointed taking my horse's reins.

I didn't spot the buck until he moved. He bolted out of the trees, ran up the trail a bit directly away from me, then cut left behind a thicket of trees. I squeezed my cow call and he stopped. I wasn't able to get a clear shot at him until he moved into a small opening above me. **BOOM!** The buck lurched, dropped and rolled down toward us until a tree stopped him.

"Nice shootin', Brady!"

"Thanks, Buck!" I walked up the slope to him with my rifle just in case he wasn't dead. He's a small three point," I said grabbing his antlers and dragging him down to the trail to field dress him.

That season was the last time, I saw the trapper's cabin. The next two seasons, we hunted to the east of Buck's ranch, and in August, prior to the upcoming season, Buck was involved in a most unfortunate horse accident. He and his neighbor, who was riding with him, stopped on a hillside near the ranch to rest their horses and take in the scenery. Buck was riding a three year old mare that he'd been training for a client. To this day, no one can figure out what spooked the mare, but she suddenly went crazy. Buck, being the excellent rider he is, attempted to stay on and ride her out rather than bail off into the hillside. In the process of being bucked, he hit the saddle horn twice which broke his pelvis in two different places. Thank God his neighbor, Don was riding with him! Don rode down to the ranch and alerted Buck's daughter, Jamie who drove the pickup and Don up to where Buck lay on the hillside. Jamie and the neighbor helped him into the truck and she drove him to St. Pat's Hospital in Missoula. When the doctors there saw that Buck had broken his pelvis in two places, they ordered him airlifted to Sacred Heart Hospital in Spokane, where there was a surgeon who could repair such breaks. The surgeon, who had to first align Buck's pelvis, placed seven screws in the front of his pelvis and one very long screw in the back to secure his pelvis to his backbone.

When Patsy and I visited him in November of that year, he'd been in a hydraulic recliner chair for over nine weeks, and dependent on crutches to move about. It would be several more weeks before he could walk without the aid of crutches. This horrific accident ended our annual hunts together, but the wonderful hunting memories we share still live on in our minds.

It's now been three years since the accident. Astonishingly, Buck is able to ride a horse again for short distances, but has difficulty getting on and off the horse. While his days of hunting on horseback are certainly over, he enjoys helping his twin granddaughters raise and train their horses. The young girls have both won many awards showing their Missouri Foxtrotters at various competitions. They carry on Buck's love and passion for raising, training and riding horses.

I still think of the trapper from time to time. I remain in awe of his toughness and perseverance, and am curious about how he arrived at the Bearmouth, found the underground spring back in Moyle, and how he built his cabin. I've done some research to find any record of him but haven't been able to find any documented information. What an historical fiction story this could make—maybe someday.

Acknowledgements

SPECIAL THANKS to my wife, Polly, who not only patiently supported my hours and hours of writing, but provided me invaluable feedback.

www.ingramcontent.com/pod-product-compliance
Lightning Source LLC
Chambersburg PA
CBHW060120260626
47160CB00005B/1959